An

Ambiguous

Tragedy

Also by Diane Eklund-Āboliņš

45 Days: Walking the Bibbulmun Track
Room Nineteen
The Space in Between: A Story about Nina

Poetry
On the Circle
Glänsande vitt på blått

An

Ambiguous

Tragedy

Diane Eklund-Āboliņš

"What we perceive around us as being real, is, on the one hand, essentially real for us in that moment of perception, and yet, at the same time, it can be completely unreal... " V.A. Collins

1

Much later, the newspapers would write that she was thirty-five, a part-time beautician married to Gregory Payne, a sales representative with Trust Us Insurance, and that she had no children. The photos accompanying the text would show that she was slight, of average height with short fair hair. The photos and the text and the television reports would attempt to bundle everything together and draw a line under what had happened, but there would always be at least one stray question or one blurred image that would refuse to remain above the line. What happened to Sandra Payne was impossible to confine: it could have happened to anyone.

***

The train had been packed, and she had no choice but to stand for most of the thirty-minute trip into Sydney's CBD. She hated being pushed up against lots of other people, especially now when it was so hot and the air conditioning was not working. When she finally alighted at the underground station, she was feeling slightly irritated. It was obvious that the transport system was inadequate: no wonder people were demanding more trains, better trains, faster trains.

She followed the crowd up the stairs and through the

ticket barrier and entered the arcade that was an extension of the underground station. A variety of shops, their windows gleaming with a profusion of colours and lights, were doing their best to coax her inside. There were people everywhere, and the air was polluted with loud music: Christmas carols that had been squeezed through some popular-music machine to emerge at the other end scarcely recognizable.

She was almost knocked over by a man completely absorbed in his phone, and when she moved to one side to avoid him she just missed being collected by a formidable wall of three young women walking arm in arm. It had not always been like this; she was sure of that. She believed that she could still remember when it had been possible to stroll through the city in one's own personal space.

But now there were so many people, and everyone was in such a dreadful hurry.

She reached a short flight of stairs that took her to a lower level: same type of shops, same rush, same noise. She noticed a tall, thin man manoeuvring a large maroon suitcase through the crowds of people. For a moment, she felt vaguely sorry for him, but then her attention was caught by a window display showing rows of brightly coloured shoes.

She thought: I really should buy some new shoes.

When she finally reached the escalator going up, it was not moving: it had stopped. It was, however, the only way to reach the street above, and although she disliked walking up (or down) non-moving escalators she stepped on to it. Halfway up she could see the man with the suitcase. Now that she was closer to him, she noticed that he had unkempt grey hair, that he was around fifty years of age and that he was wearing a nondescript beige coloured summer suit and a purple shirt. It was obvious that he was not at all happy about having to carry the suitcase up the escalator when he had most probably been expecting a relatively easy ride. At the top, he placed the suitcase on the ground, pulled up the handle, and, with the weight of the case now resting on the small black wheels, he quickly disappeared around the corner of the building and into the sea of people outside.

Sandra followed the man away from the escalator, moved to the left of the footpath and adjusted her speed to those around her. She would have preferred to have sauntered but that was completely out of the question: she would have been mowed down in an instant. When she saw the bookshop, she dived across the oncoming crush of pedestrians and headed for the open door.

***

Inside the shop, the air-conditioned coolness was a relief after the heat outside. She breathed in the synthetic, fresh smell of new books and moved to a table that was further from the door. It was piled with discounted books that Sandra recognized as having once been bestsellers. She picked up one of the books and turned it over to read the blurb on the back. Her mind, however, was elsewhere, and after reading a couple of sentences she returned the book to the table and moved on.

The eager young man in the crisp white shirt and dark tie smiled at her as she approached the information desk. He listened politely as he tapped the details into his computer and then scrolled down the screen. The smile waned a little as he slowly shook his head and said that the book she was looking for seemed to be out of stock. But he was there to help, so he suggested that she ask his colleague on the first floor; there was always a small chance that they might still have one copy left. 'Straight up the escalator and then turn left,' he said, his smile once more firmly in place.

Thankfully the escalator was moving.

As she was about to step on to the bottom step, she heard the wail of sirens. The sound was very loud and came to an abrupt halt outside the shop. Several people put down the books they were holding and moved towards the door. A wave of uncertainty swept through the shop. Someone said that a man had been killed, knocked down by a bus.

For a moment Sandra was almost inclined to join the small scattered procession of people moving towards the door, but then she stopped herself and stepped on to the escalator. Part of her could agree that the need many people had to gawk at the misfortune of others was completely macabre. Was it morbid curiosity, or was it simply a feeble attempt to ensure that such a thing would not happen to them? She was not sure.

At the top of the escalator, she turned to the left. She had no idea where to look for the book and sought the help of an assistant.

'Virtual Reality and Abstract Truth,' said the assistant, tapping in the title on one of the computer stations. She looked at the screen and then at Sandra. 'Sorry,' she said, 'nothing in store at the moment, but I could order it for you. It wouldn't be here until after Christmas though.'

Sandra nodded. She had hoped to give it to Greg for Christmas; it was actually the reason she had taken that awful train into the city. Now she would have to do a rethink. She was disappointed, because Greg had been talking about the book for weeks, and she had wanted to surprise him. There was nothing to do about it, he would have to wait.

She gave the girl her details and returned to the lower level of the shop. So far her day had been a definite failure; she would have a coffee and then she would decide what to do. Perhaps she would buy some new shoes.

***

Outside the shop, the ambulance was just pulling away, and a small group of curious bystanders was beginning to disperse. Two policemen were interviewing a rather nervous-looking teenager and an elderly couple. Witnesses, no doubt. Sandra looked past the policemen to the edge of the footpath where a large maroon suitcase was standing as if abandoned.

So, it was the man from the escalator - someone she knew. Well, not exactly *knew*, but she *had* seen him, walked behind him, even thought about him (if somewhat briefly). For some reason, she felt a strange sense of loss. Should she mention to the police that she almost knew him? She discarded the thought even before it had settled properly in her mind and decided that what she needed was some strong coffee.

She found a small coffee place tucked in between a homewares shop, with a nineteenth-century façade, and a modern building that seemed to be nothing but glass held together by steel supports. She ordered a double espresso, found a vacant table in a reasonably secluded corner and, while she drank her coffee, studied the furnishings and thought about the man with the maroon suitcase. It was strange that she should have seen him, not once but twice, and that he should have then died so tragically, but the more she thought about it the less strange it became. The fact that he had stood out from the crowd because of his suitcase hardly meant that she had a special connection with him. She saw lots of people every day, and it was more than possible that many people she had once seen were now dead. The connection was tenuous to say the least.

A large blue ceramic clock on the bright yellow wall behind the cash register showed that it was almost noon. She left the café, deciding to look for shoes before taking the train home. The shoe shops, like most other shops, were packed, and she could not find exactly what she was looking for, so after a frustrating half an hour she decided to forget about new shoes and head for the station.

Standing on the escalator, travelling down to her platform, she was startled to see the man with his maroon suitcase riding on the up escalator. As far as she knew he should have been fighting for his life in a hospital somewhere, if he was not already lying in the morgue; obviously she had misunderstood something. But, if he was not the man run down by the bus, why had his suitcase been standing at the scene, alone and abandoned? There was something strange about it all. Or was there? She really did not know, but she did feel as though she was beginning to lose any hold on reality that she may have previously thought she had.

As they passed, the man looked at her and almost smiled. It was simply the vacant, neutral smile of one person on an up escalator passing another person on a down escalator, but she still felt that she needed to grab hold of the rail to steady herself.

On the platform she made an impulsive, if somewhat

insane and completely illogical, decision: she had to find out who he was and why he was still alive. She had a vague feeling in the pit of her stomach that she was going to regret her decision, but she needed some answers. The social complications of approaching someone and asking him why he was alive and not dead had not yet fully occurred to her. She stepped on to the escalator and quickly disappeared up towards the concourse.

2

The last straggling houses were behind him, and he was already surrounded by paddocks. There was a wide, unsealed shoulder on each side of the road, beyond which narrow, fairly irregular, lines of blue-grey eucalyptus trees partly obscured barbed-wire fences. In parts he could see that the wire had broken away from the posts and was trailing or coiling on the ground. Further away there was only dry colourless grass and the occasional solitary eucalyptus tree.

He drove for another three or four kilometres until he noticed a substantial area of bush: a conglomeration of trees and thick scrub climbing a rise on the right-hand side of the road. He immediately did a U-turn and parked the small blue rental car off the road, beyond the shoulder. As he stepped out of the car, he became aware of the overpowering sound of cicadas and other insects, sounds which seemed to magnify the word *summer*. He was thankfully aware that the oppressive heat of earlier in the day had all but disappeared.

He opened the back door and removed his camera from the seat. Then he locked the car and stepped on to a rough track that ran at a ninety-degree angle away from the road and towards the rise.

The medium-sized rural country town, situated on a wide flat below a range of small rounded hills, was one of the towns west of the Great Dividing Range that Greg usually visited several times a year. With the plethora of present-day communication possibilities, there was much that could be organized directly from head office, but Greg knew that face-to-face interaction was vitally important. Moreover, he enjoyed the change of scenery.

He had spent two days in the town, and he was booked on a regional flight back to Sydney early the following morning. Everything had gone well: the office, with a number of new initiatives and several new clients, was functioning beyond his expectations.

As he stepped on to the track, which led up into the hills, he was aware that beyond the hills the land flattened out towards the west as far as the eye could see. That was the reason he was here: to capture an image of the setting sun.

***

Greg was thinking of Sandra as he walked. He had last spoken to her that morning, and she had mentioned something about taking the train into the city. He was also thinking about the previous evening at the pub – three of the fellows from the office and himself. It was while they were at the pub that Doug had suggested the view from the end of Shane's track: 'Great sunsets. Great views. Flat as far as you can see.'

Doug knew that Greg was an amateur photographer.

The other two had nodded and had then continued to drink their beer. Not that they were really interested in photography, but they both agreed about the flatness, and they could accept that an unbroken expanse of red and pink and purple dipping down to spread over the unbroken earth was something special, or, as Evans put it: 'Awesome; bloody awesome.'

Doug's eyes had been fixed on the glass in his hand when he said, 'Follow Shane's track to the very end; that's where you'll get the best view.'

The conversation meandered off in another direction, but eventually looped back to Shane's track when Greg wondered about the name. It was then that Doug mentioned that a man named Shane had disappeared somewhere near the track. 'It must have been at least five years ago, and he hasn't been seen anywhere since,' he said. 'Perhaps he *wanted* to disappear, no one knows for certain.'

Evans had only been living in the town for six months. He had moved there from northern New South Wales after completing the insurance certificate that he hoped would set him on a new path. He had not heard anything about anyone disappearing, but he could understand someone *needing* to disappear – for Evans, disappearing was really no big deal.

Greg, on the other hand, had a strange, uncomfortable feeling in the pit of his stomach. Perhaps taking photos of sunsets was no longer a number-one priority.

***

Shane Lachlan had lived on the edge of the town. He did odd jobs and occasionally picked up work on the surrounding properties. He used to get around in an old green ute with his dog, Alf, standing on the tray at the back. Then on a summer's day about five years ago Alf turned up in town minus Shane. The people who knew Alf realized that something was wrong, because Shane and his dog were inseparable. The police did some checking and discovered that Shane had been working on a property about ten kilometres south-west of the town but that he had finished the job around three the previous afternoon and had then packed up and left.

'The police searched the whole ten kilometres of road,' Doug continued, 'and they finally found his ute a short way in along Shane's track.'

Brian added, 'It wasn't called Shane's track then... '

'Not then, but later... ' Doug said, 'they wanted to do something to remember him, you know how it is?'

Shane's box of assorted tools and an old waterproof jacket were still in the tray, and there were eleven dollars and twenty-five cents in the glove box. The keys were still in the ignition. Nothing made any sense.

The police searched the surrounding area without finding anything that could explain what had happened to Shane. It was as though he had simply evaporated. A sniffer dog managed to follow Shane's scent to the end of the track, and the police wondered if perhaps Shane had fallen from the ridge. A new search was initiated and police and volunteers fanned out across the ridge all the way down to the plains, but there was no sign of Shane. Not anywhere.

Someone suggested that Shane may have needed to disappear, but the suggestion was shelved early in the investigation. Shane's way of life might have seemed rather serendipitous, but the police could find no indication of financial stress or scorned, revengeful women. It was also argued that Shane would not have voluntarily disappeared and left Alf behind. There were too many questions and no answers. The only thing that was certain was that Shane had completely vanished. Whether he had died as a result of an accident, whether he had been killed or whether he was still alive was anyone's guess.

They finished their beer.

'Don't forget that photo,' Doug said as they all left the pub.

The feeling in Greg's stomach was becoming more pronounced by the minute.

***

However, after a good night's sleep everything looked and felt very different in the warm, bright sunlight, and Greg decided that he would take a trip out to Shane's track after he was finished in the office. It would be a shame to pass up such a wonderful photo opportunity.

Initially the track was fairly easy going, but it became rougher and narrower as it began to climb into the hills. Prickly bushes and dry grasses fought with gnarled eucalyptus trees for space, while many large rocky outcrops caused the track to loop and wind back on itself. In places the track dropped several metres, almost without warning, before picking itself up and climbing even more steeply.

Greg pushed on. He was not much of a walker, and he found the many ascents and descents, together with a multitude of very small, irritating black flies, extremely trying. Several times he saw wallabies on the track, but before he could aim his camera they disappeared into the undergrowth. He was not overly disappointed; he was saving all his creative enthusiasm for the prize at the end of the track.

A couple of times he thought he may have heard sounds: snapping twigs, sliding stones, footsteps... but he reminded himself of the wallabies and other creatures in the bush and told himself that he had to keep his imagination in check. Now was definitely not a good time to let his fears run riot.

He reached the top of the ridge just as the first long lines of pink were stretching across the sky. The view was unbelievable and definitely worth the trek. He sat down on a boulder, his camera in his hand. From where he sat he could see how the ridge dropped down to the vast plain in front of him: a sea of grey and brown stretching as far as he could see.

The sun was dipping towards the horizon. The sky was colouring quickly, and it was very quiet.

Then he thought he heard footsteps. And voices.

He decided to take notice of what might turn out to be an overwrought imagination, and he squeezed himself behind the boulder and then scrambled further along the ridge. He did not stop until he found a large outcrop of rocks partially covered with vegetation. Although the full panorama of the sunset was now somewhat obstructed, he had a fairly good view of the track, and he would be able to see if anyone was following him.

His disappointment at not being able to take the perfect photo was completely swept away by an overwhelming feeling of anxiety. He could not stop thinking of Shane Lachlan. Had he actually been murdered, or had he simply missed his footing somewhere along the ridge? Perhaps his body was still caught between rocks where no one had thought to look, or perhaps he was actually alive, enjoying a new life in a new town.

The sunset, or what he could see of it, was magnificent. No one appeared along the track, and he heard no more sounds. Obviously, he had been spooked by the story about Shane. He decided to move back to what he regarded as the viewing area and take his photo. The sky was already beginning to darken a little, and he knew that there was was not much time left if he wanted a reasonably good photo.

Then he heard the footsteps again, and he also picked up the vague smell of cigarette smoke. He drew back behind the rocks.

As he stood there with the sky darkening around him, he wondered if he were not being a trifle ridiculous. Perhaps the people (whoever they might be) were simply people like himself who had come out to look at the sunset. Looking at the situation realistically, he decided that the chances of someone actually wanting to abduct him, or kill him, were extremely remote.

Part of him wanted to return to the track; the other part was reluctant. In the end it was the other part that won. A breeze blew up, and it became dark. He found it difficult to see his immediate environment much less the track. He could hear voices, and he guessed that the people who owned those voices were now at the viewing area. The smell of smoke was closer and more obvious.

He tried to hear what was being said, but it was impossible. He wondered if ordinary people stood on bush tracks in the dark, smoking and talking, but his thoughts always came back to the same question: Why were they there if they were not looking for him?

They did not seem to be in any great hurry to leave. Perhaps they knew that he was there, and they were simply waiting for him to show himself. He heard them laughing: was it at a joke one of them had told, or was it because they knew that they had the upper hand? Greg was worried that the anxiety was completely unhinging him. In all probability there was a perfectly reasonable explanation for the men being where they were.

Greg was, however, not prepared to show himself. The darkness became even darker and a couple of owls filled the sound space that the other birds and insects had vacated. He became aware that the voices had stopped and that the smell of smoke had drifted away. The men had almost certainly left.

"Almost certainly" were, however, the two words that Greg could not let go of. He could not believe that the men had actually left: they were probably hiding further back along the track. He knew that he would have to stay where he was: not only was it dark and the track, in parts, was relatively dangerous, but there was also the possibility of his meeting up with the men. There was nothing to do about it; he would have to stay put. He settled himself in a wedge between the rocks to wait out the night.

***

Very early in the morning, as soon as the light began to return, Greg stood up and stretched himself. He had barely slept; he felt stiff and he desperately wanted a shower, a shave, a change of clothes and a cup of very strong coffee. Shouldering his camera, he began the walk back to the car.

Although it was a beautiful morning with the new sun glistening on leaves, and the birds waking up after a night of silence, Greg was not in the right mood to be appreciative. He was still not sure whether he had been a complete idiot or whether someone had actually been following him. He doubted that there was any way he would ever be able to find out.

As he neared the end of the track, he was relieved to see that his car was still standing where he had left it. Next to the car, on the ground, were several cigarette butts, so perhaps he had not been imagining things after all.

He unlocked the car, lowered himself into the driver's seat, put the key in the ignition, indicated and pulled out on to the road.

***

At the hotel, he had a quick shower, changed his clothes and packed. Outside, on the footpath, he ran into Doug, who asked him, 'Did you get out to Shane's track?'

Greg wondered if he detected something sinister lurking behind the question, but he quickly decided that he was being hypersensitive. He shook his head with a wry smile. 'That's a long story; I'll tell you about it some-time,' he said.

On the plane, during the flight back to Sydney, his mind was still trying to find a logical explanation for what had happened. Did the people on the track have some ulterior, unpleasant reason for being there, or were they, like himself, simply interested in the view? Or was it a case of the boys from the office pulling his leg?

Then he suddenly remembered: none of the boys who had been at the pub with him smoked.

3

Doug, a couple of years younger than Greg, had always lived in the country. He had been born there, went to school there, and to his utmost relief had been able to find work there. He had been working with Trust Us Insurance for the past six years, and the work suited him. While Greg was responsible for the contact between the Sydney office and the medium-sized office in the town, Doug travelled regularly to all the smaller towns in the district. He enjoyed the travel, he enjoyed meeting people, and, most of all, he enjoyed being able to live in the country.

He had gone to school with Shane. Admittedly Shane had been two or three classes ahead of Doug, but the two boys had been aware of each other's existence, and after they had finished school they occasionally saw each other at social or sporting events. It was, after all, only a middle-sized town.

They never became close friends; in fact they never really moved beyond the superficial greetings that form that tenuous link between people who say 'Yes, I know so-and-so,' where the verb *know* is not much more than a collection of four letters without much content. But when Shane disappeared, Doug had been devastated.

Later, when he thought about it, he decided that he would have been devastated no matter who had disappeared in such a way without explanation. That he was *so* devastated probably stemmed from the fact that he and Shane were roughly the same age and had lived all their lives in the same town, sharing many of the same spaces and mixing with many of the same people.

While the townspeople were wondering how such a dreadful thing could have happened to such a nice young man, Doug suspected that there had to be more behind the whole business than either the police or the media were reporting. It was rumoured that Shane may have owed someone money, and Doug vaguely wondered if that could be the link.

Because there was no body, there could be no funeral, no proper farewell. Even though it was not certain that Shane was dead, the people in the town needed something to put an end (*closure* was the word they used) to Shane's disappearance. After much debate, they decided to hold a small celebration of Shane's life in the town park, and, to put a distance between Shane's possible demise and the chance that he was still alive, they selected the mayor of the town to conduct the ceremony. The Anglican minister said a short prayer, and then the mayor spoke of Shane's contribution to the community and how everyone was praying (at which point he looked across to the minister) for Shane's safe return. Doug was not sure what contribution Shane had made, but he certainly wanted him to turn up again, safe and sound.

Time passed, but Shane did not turn up. Weeks turned into months and soon a whole year had slipped away without any sign of Shane, dead or alive. The police and a couple of forensic scientists scrounged the area, looking for clues. A couple of possible leads fizzled out, and eventually everyone just seemed to lose interest. The forensic scientists packed up their instruments and disappeared; the local newspaper lost interest; life moved on. Some people believed that Shane had fallen from the ridge and that his body had been eaten by feral animals; a few believed that he had moved interstate. Doug was more inclined to agree with the latter, but no one had any evidence either way.

Almost two years after Shane's disappearance, a couple of German backpackers arrived in the town. They spent the night at a youth hostel not far from the railway station, and in the morning they told the hostel proprietor that they were intending to hitch-hike at least one hundred kilometres south-west. The proprietor wished them luck, after which neither he nor anyone else gave them very much thought: backpackers and tourists passed through the town all the time.

Three months later the police received a call from the Department of Foreign Affairs in Canberra. Did they possibly have any knowledge of two Germans, Hans Neumann and Friedrich Keller, who may have passed through the town some months back? The two boys, both in their early twenties, had not been in touch with their parents for weeks, and the parents were under-standably concerned. The German Ministry of Foreign Affairs had contacted its Embassy in Canberra, and slowly the web of concern had grown to contain several departments and a host of different people. The media was involved with articles in both the print and online versions of their newspapers, while on television there were interviews with departmental staff and even with the parents. Had anyone anywhere seen these two boys? Information slowly began to trickle in, and eventually a circle was drawn around the name of the town. All reports concerning the boys seemed to finish at that particular town. Perhaps the answer to the boys' disappearance was somewhere there?

The police swung into action and finally tracked down the proprietor of the hostel where the boys had stayed. They now had something specific to work with – the boys had taken the south-west road – and the police moved their investigations to another town one hundred kilometres away. Every possibility and even a number of impossibilities were taken into consideration and studied, but eventually everyone had to concede that the boys had most probably never reached their destination. The police then turned their attention to the long stretch of road between the two towns.

It was a couple of weeks after the investigation had begun when a William Boyd phoned the police with what he hoped might be helpful information regarding the German boys. At first he was reluctant to give his name as he did not want to be drawn into something that actually had nothing to do with him, but the police were not interested in any information that could not be authenticated.

William said that he had seen the boys on the day in question, on the road running south from the town. When he saw them, they were already a couple of kilometres beyond the town and were obviously hoping to get a lift. William added that he would have picked them up, but he was heading into the town not away from it. He had remembered the boys because, when he caught a glimpse of them in his rear-view mirror, he noticed that one of them had a large German flag across the back of his backpack.

The police began to work southwards from the point where William Boyd had seen them, and two kilometres further along the road, they came to Shane's track. The officer-in-charge had been involved in the search for

Shane Lachlan a couple of years earlier, and he decided that although that particular search had been fruitless they should still check the track even though it was on the opposite side of the road.

They had almost reached the viewing area and were preparing to admit that it had all been a waste of time, when a small flash of red and yellow between two large brown-grey boulders caught their attention. When they inspected it closer, they saw that it was an almost empty backpack that had been pushed into a very small space.

They had traced the Germans to Shane's track.

Over the next few weeks, the area around the track was filled with police, forensic scientists, media, embassy officials and, finally, the parents of the two boys, all four of whom had flown out from Germany to find out what had happened to their sons. Everyone was hoping for a positive result, but as with Shane Lachlan the trail stopped at Shane's track. There was nothing that gave any indication as to what had happened to the two boys.

After a month of praying and hoping, the parents left two wreaths near the boulders, and on the advice of their embassy returned home. The police marked the case as unsolved, and the media devoted its attention to other, newer topics.

***

Eighteen months later, on a Tuesday morning in June, Betsy Riley phoned her sister Thelma, who lived on a property forty kilometres outside the town. Betsy, a woman in her mid-sixties, had business to attend to in a town further south, but it was not much of a detour to call by her sister's place, and, if it suited Thelma, she could stay overnight.

When Betsy failed to arrive after several hours, Thelma unsuccessfully tried to phone her sister's landline and then her mobile. Not sure what she should do next, but fearing the worst, she finally contacted the police. Perhaps Betsy had been taken ill and was unable to come to the phone? Perhaps there had been an accident?

The following day the car was found – it had broken down almost level with Shane's track – but there was no sign of Betsy Riley. The police decided that she may have tried to walk back to town, and they searched the entire length of road. Betsy was nowhere to be found.

There was, of course, no indication that Betsy's disappearance had anything at all to do with Shane's track, but the townspeople began avoiding it. Most of them argued that it was far better to be safe than sorry.

Doug knew that he should have given Greg the whole story about Shane's track that evening in the pub, and he had no idea why he had only mentioned Shane. Perhaps it was because there was no direct proof that the track had anything to do with the disappearance of the Germans or Betsy Riley or, for that matter, even Shane Lachlan. Doug desperately wanted everyone to move on after five years, and the only way they could do that was to believe that the track was no different and no more dangerous than any of the other surrounding areas.

**

But later, after they had all left the pub, Doug became increasingly concerned over his omission to tell Greg the whole story. Although he tried to assure himself that he had done the right thing, he wondered just how sensible it was, sending someone out to a site where four people had disappeared. He tried to blame his over-sight on the fact that he had been drinking and that his powers of reasoning may have been somewhat com-promised, but he knew that it had nothing to do with his drinking and more to do with his own personal per-spective. Nevertheless, had it been possible to relive that hour in the pub, he was certain that he would have acted differently: he would have been more honest. While he was thinking about what he could have done or what he should have done, he was only too aware that the evening, like every second of time that was now in the past, was completely irretrievable.

The following day he decided he would say something to Greg – he would tell him to forget about the photo – but an unexpected job came up early in the morning, and he was away all day with a client in a neighbouring town. By the time he returned, Greg had already left.

He tried to allay his anxiety and concerns by main-taining that superstitions, like those surrounding Shane's track, would simply snowball out of all proportion unless people were prepared to look at the facts in a logical manner. He told himself that that is all he had been trying to do; someone had to be brave enough to step beyond the rumours and the scaremongering. Still and all, he spent a very anxious, sleepless night, wondering whether or not he would ever see Greg again. His relief when he saw him outside the hotel the following morning was indescribable. He was convinced that a man about to be hanged but reprieved at the last moment could not have felt more relieved than he did.

While he tried not to show the relief he felt, he remembered Greg looking at him rather strangely and saying something about a long story.

Doug wondered if he would ever hear that story.

4

On the train home, Sandra's thoughts kept circling in and out of the events of the last couple of hours. She could not understand why she had behaved in such a manner: she was definitely not an impulsive person; she always thought things through very carefully before deciding on a course of action.

She would have liked to have been able to erase the image of herself on the escalator, chasing after a man she did not even know, but it was impossible. That image remained even as another image – herself on the concourse – pushed to the forefront of her mind. The man was nowhere to be seen, and it was at this point that she should have given up and returned to the platform. Still hoping to get a glimpse of the man, she had pushed through the crowds and hurried from ticket barrier to ticket barrier, until it slowly dawned on her that he was no longer there. Finally she had had no choice but to admit defeat, and she had then taken the escalator back down to her platform.

She wondered what it was about the man that could have caused her to act in such a way.

Standing on the platform, waiting for her train, she felt that she had been an idiot. She hoped that no one had noticed her impulsive chase up the escalator, and her cheeks blushed as she considered the possibility of someone watching her and, which was completely im-possible, understanding what she had been doing.

It was a relief to be on the train; she would do her best to forget the man with the suitcase, and she would focus on other things. She thought about Greg and even considered phoning him, but then she realized that he would be working, so she returned her phone to her handbag and gazed out of the window instead.

***

Greg returned to Sydney late the following morning, and as it was a Saturday he did not go to the office but came straight on home. Sandra was concerned that he was quieter than usual. When she asked him about his trip his answers were short, and they did not invite further questions. She felt slightly snubbed, but she decided that he was probably tired. On some level, she could accept that he possibly did not want to talk about work, but she was still feeling stressed about her experience the previous day, and she needed some confirmation of his closeness if not his understanding. In the circum-stances, she decided not to mention the man with the suitcase: the less said about her trip to the city the better.

Christmas came and went. The old year turned into a new year, and people made resolutions to be better, more efficient and kinder, knowing that the resolutions, like the new year, would soon fade into ordinariness, and life would resume its old path.

At the end of January, Sandra received a letter from the bookshop apologizing for the delay in getting back to her - there had been a problem with the publisher - but the book, *Virtual Reality and Abstract Truth,* was now in the shop, and she was welcome to collect it whenever convenient.

At the same time, Greg discovered that he needed to make an extra trip back to the country town he had visited prior to Christmas, the new year having brought with it changes to the regulations regarding property insurance applications. Seeing the chance for a short break, they both applied for a few days off from work: they would drive out to the country town, and after Greg finished his business at the office they would drive on to Canberra and spend a couple of days in the capital.

Sandra decided that she would collect the book on their return.

***

While Greg was at the office, Sandra had a late breakfast at the hotel where they were staying, and then she went for a walk around the town. After wandering in and out of a number of shops, the décor and the merchandise transporting her backwards at least half a century, she climbed a small hill, lined with maples, from where both the Catholic and Anglican churches looked out over the town. She paused for some minutes outside the Anglican church, enjoying the view, absorbing the patterns of the town bordered by the flatness beyond.

For no particular reason she suddenly thought about the man with the suitcase. The thought disturbed her; she had wanted to forget him. She was not sure why, but she definitely wanted him relegated to her past.

Forcing herself to think of other things, she continued past the churches and down the other side of the hill towards the town park: a substantial expanse of green grass with a variety of large trees and a scattering of flower beds. When she reached the east gate, an un-assuming construction of black wrought-iron set into the low stone wall, she unlatched it and walked inside. Greg had mentioned the park to her on their drive from Sydney, and he had even suggested it to her before he left the hotel that morning. She knew that it had four wrought-iron gates and that it was completely enclosed by a stone wall. 'Built by convicts,' Greg had told her.

She also remembered something about a children's play area, a pond, which had been constructed by dam-ming a small creek that flowed through the area, a bandstand and a war memorial.

She followed the path to the pond where she found a wooden bench under a large Moreton Bay fig. She sat down on the bench and opened the book she had brought with her, but there was too much around her that was demanding her attention: the sun dancing through the leaves of the enormous tree, the roses in the garden bed beyond where she was sitting, the ducks on the edge of the pond. She closed the book, and almost immediately her thoughts returned to the man with the suitcase. She was still wondering why she kept thinking about him, when Greg phoned. He told her that every-thing had gone well and that he would meet her back at the hotel in fifteen minutes.

***

It was a beautiful day, and the sky was completely blue without the trace of a cloud. For some reason, Sandra's spirits had lifted considerably, and although the man with the suitcase cut across her thoughts a couple of times she no longer felt that it was anything to worry about. She was looking forward to spending a couple of days in Canberra; she had absolutely no intention of letting anyone with a suitcase spoil them for her.

A few kilometres beyond the town, Greg suddenly did a U-turn, pulled off the road and parked. Sandra glanced at him in surprise. There was nothing of significance anywhere, at least not that she could see: a wide swathe of bush pushing its way up a hill and a couple of crows sitting on a barbed-wire fence. She anxiously wondered if he had forgotten something or if there was something wrong with the car.

Greg shook his head.

Sandra knew nothing about the track and nothing about what had happened there. She had no inkling of her husband's imagination running away with him that evening before Christmas. She could not know that this was a case of Greg wanting to right something inside himself. She did not know that it was something that Greg felt he had to do.

As he opened the car door Greg said, 'There's a great view from the top of those hills.'

Sandra was about to say that she was not really dressed for walking through the bush, but she thought better of it. From the boot of the car, she took out a pair of running shoes and changed from her high-heeled sandals. Then Greg locked the car and pocketed the keys, and they began to walk along the track away from the road.

It was not too hot, the flies were not as irritating as they could have been, and Sandra decided that perhaps it was not such a silly idea after all. When they reached the top of the ridge, after about thirty minutes' walking, she was delighted by the view. They sat on some rocks and rested while their eyes took in the panorama below.

It was very quiet, but it was still several hours until

sunset, so there would be no photo of coloured skies. For sometime they sat in silence, contemplating the scene before them, then Sandra stood up and walked to the edge of the ridge. She was pleased that she had not said no to the walk: it had actually been a positive experience. Below her, she could see a narrow track that wended its way down between the rocks before disappearing behind a clump of small trees. She called out to Greg that she would not be long, and she carefully began the climb down from the ridge. It was not quite as steep as she had expected, and the track itself was reasonably easy to follow. As she put more and more distance between herself and the ridge, the more relaxed she became, and she soon found herself enjoying the sensation of being completely on her own, surrounded only by bush and birds. When she reached the clump of trees, she looked up to see Greg in the distance, still sitting on the rock. She waved at him and then kept walking.

***

After about ten minutes, Greg looked at his watch and decided that they should be getting back to the car. He called out to Sandra; when there was no answer, he walked to the edge and looked down the track.

She was nowhere to be seen.

***

Anxiety flowed through Greg's body as he grappled with the realization that Sandra was not there. In spite of the warm day, he felt cold. There was tumult in the pit of his stomach, and he could feel a pressure in his head, almost as though steel clamps were being screwed tighter and tighter. For a brief moment, he was unable to breathe. He gulped in some air and called her name several times and then began climbing down the ridge. His hands were shaking, and he was trying to move faster than the track would allow, with the result that he stumbled several times. When he reached the clump of trees, he was hoping that he would be able to see her further down the ridge, but beyond the trees the empty track simply continued around the side of the ridge.

His body felt numb, and a wave of dizziness caused him to clutch at a sapling while he tried to retain his balance. He sat down for a moment, his head in his hands. By now he was feeling physically ill, and he kept asking himself why on earth he had come back to such a place. Surely his first experience should have been sufficient to have kept him away. The anxiety was beginning to overpower him. All he could think of was finding Sandra.

The track continued downwards around the ridge, and Greg had to watch his footing carefully so as not to trip. When he next looked up he saw ahead of him a small timber hut with a corrugated iron roof. The building appeared lonely and abandoned, and there was no sign of anyone anywhere. He was obviously looking at the back of the hut, but the track curved around the side of the building, and he guessed that it then passed the front of the hut before, in all probability, carrying on down the ridge.

He had guessed correctly, and when he reached the front he discovered that the door was half open. Buoyed with the hope of possibly finding Sandra inside, he pushed the door open and walked in.

It was a simple one-room dwelling with an earthen

floor and a timber bench pushed against one wall; there was even a fireplace with a blackened hearth. One of the two windows was covered with a nondescript fabric that looked as though it might have been used as a cleaning rag in its past life; the other window, at the back of the building, was minus its glass and looked blindly out on to the track he had just walked down.

A completely abandoned, empty shack.

He looked around quickly, hoping to find anything at all that might give him some idea where Sandra might be. Then his eyes fell on the bench, and he thought he recognized something lying at the far end. When he came closer, he saw that it was the green and white wrapper of a chewing gum that Sandra often used.

A chewing-gum wrapper but no sign of Sandra.

By now, Greg's anxiety had well and truly moved to centre stage. He picked up the wrapper and went back outside. He called Sandra's name several times before taking out his phone and dialling his wife's number.

There was no signal.

He looked around him in desperation and wondered what on earth he was going to do.

5

The police arrived first, only a few minutes before the Emergency Service. Greg showed everyone where he had last seen Sandra, and then he pointed out the hut. The police talked with each other in short sentences, and the volunteers from the Emergency Service spread out in a line across the ridge, their bright yellow uniforms conspicuous against the greens and the browns of the landscape. With so many people combing the area, Greg felt that his wife had to be found; it was just a matter of time.

As he stood outside the hut for the second time that day, it was as though some kind of boundary had been drawn up between what had been and what now was, and there was no way of returning to what had been. He could not rid himself of the overwhelming anxiety he had felt when he first realized that Sandra had disappeared. He remembered the distress that had filled his body at that moment of realization, part of his brain telling him to raise the alarm and another part insisting that he stay where he was. In case she came back. In case he was simply imagining it all and she was suddenly to reappear. Perhaps she had just walked off out of sight, and in all probability she would soon be back.

But after fifteen minutes of trying to will himself into two places at once, Greg became more and more certain that he would have to get help. He tore a page from his notebook, wrote a couple of lines telling Sandra where he was and then fixed the note to a rusty nail sticking out from the shed door. After yet another quick search beyond the shed, he climbed back up on to the ridge and made his way back to the car, stumbling over rocks and tree stumps, slipping and sliding on the uneven ground, driven all the time by an unease, bordering on panic, that was threatening to paralyse him.

The place that before had been so secluded and quiet was now the complete opposite. There were people everywhere. If Sandra was anywhere at all out there, she would have to hear the noise, see the people. Greg concentrated all his energy on willing her to see something, hear something.

He was jolted from his concentration by a police officer wanting to check Sandra's movements with him. Yet again. Yes, she had been up on the ridge with him, and then she had walked down the track. He had not seen her since.

**

Doug touched him on the shoulder. Greg turned, surprised to see his colleague there.

'I had to come,' said Doug. 'If there is anything I can do... ' His voice faded off. He was quiet for a moment, and then he said, 'You know, I hate to say it, but it's sort of my fault.'

Greg looked at him incredulously.

Doug told him about the German tourists and Betsy Riley. He was extremely upset. He said that he should have said something earlier, but it had not been definitely proved that the track had anything to do with their disappearance.

'I was trying to see it all in perspective; I wanted to ignore the rumours and the assumptions,' he faltered, 'but I was wrong; I know that now. I should have said something to you.'

While a torrent of different emotions rushed through him, Greg simply stood there, shaking his head; he did not trust himself to say anything. Hearing that other people, not just Shane, had disappeared from the track came as a dreadful shock, but he could not really blame Doug. Knowing what had happened to Shane should have been sufficient to have kept him well away from the place. Though perhaps had he known of the others he would most definitely have hesitated about returning. And certainly not with Sandra.

Later, at the police station, there were the questions. 'Not that we believe you did anything,' said the middle-aged detective, clicking the top of his ballpoint pen incessantly, 'it's all just part of our procedure. You do understand, don't you?'

Greg had nodded, not really understanding. All he wanted was for someone to find Sandra. While he sat in the small office at the station, he was imagining an interruption to the interview: an officer knocking at the door with the information that she had been found. That she was safe and well.

The man was talking again.'You both get along okay? No problems that we need to know about?'

The dream disintegrated, and the pieces flew around the room. Greg decided that the question was intrusive, but the whole business with the interview was intrusive. Had things gone to plan, they would have been well on their way to Canberra by now. He grimaced and wondered why Sandra had wandered off. Just then. But while he was feeling irritated with Sandra for disappearing, he was feeling even more irritated with himself for stopping at the track.

'Definitely not,' he answered, unable to completely hide the irritation he was feeling. Like his dream, he felt as though he himself was disintegrating. He wondered if he would ever be able to collect together all the pieces. If she did not return. If no one was able to find her.

The man in front of Greg closed his notebook. 'Thank you, Mr Payne. We'll be in touch with you if we need to talk again.'

Gregory was still hoping for that interruption. He took the man's outstretched hand, knowing that as far as the police were concerned he was most probably the only suspect.

'I can assure you, I didn't cause my wife to disappear,' he ventured, a touch of tired sarcasm in his voice.

The detective shrugged and indicated that Greg was free to go.

***

For the next week, the police searched the site but found no further clues. The chewing-gum wrapper had been carefully bagged and labelled and was, as far as Greg knew, the only piece of evidence to date. The Emergency Service volunteers were joined by a group from the local bushwalking club, and together they explored every centimetre of the ridge and then scoured kilometres of the plain below.

There was no sign of Sandra anywhere.

Unable to remain at the hotel, doing nothing, Greg occasionally joined the bushwalkers or went off on short forays of his own, all the time rebuking himself for having been so stupid. A couple of times he stopped by at the office, but he found everyone's sympathetic looks and muted conversations difficult to cope with. Head office reassured him that he could take off as much time as he needed; everyone was thinking of him and, of course, Sandra.

Whereas Shane had merited a celebration of his life in the town park, and the German tourists had been remembered by their parents at the place of their disappearance, Betsy Riley's family had refused any kind of ceremony, claiming that it would merely confirm that she was dead; as far as they were concerned she was simply missing, assumed living.

Doug was not sure what to do about Sandra. In the circumstances, he was uncomfortable about the idea of giving Greg flowers, but he felt that the office needed to do something to show its sympathy and support. In the end it was decided to give him a card, and the task of purchasing the card was bestowed on Jocelyn, the eighteen-year-old office junior. With its white lilies and gold cross on a purple background, it was perhaps not exactly what the others had had in mind; however, everyone added their signature, and Greg thanked them all for their support and said that he was still optimistic that Sandra would be found alive and well.

The police interviewed him again, on two separate occasions, but finally concluded that they had no reason to suspect him of any kind of criminal activity towards his wife, and his name was removed from their list.

After two very stagnant, frustrating weeks, Greg decided that there was no point in staying in the town any longer, and he returned to Sydney.

***

He had not been prepared for how dreadful it would be, coming back to an empty house where everything reminded him of Sandra. His older sister wanted him to move in with them, but although part of him craved company another part needed to be completely alone. He felt as though he was in a kind of limbo zone where it was impossible to move positively in any direction. He was constantly walking a tightrope between hope and despair. He developed a number of obsessive-compulsive characteristics, believing that if he did things in a certain order, answered the phone after a certain number of rings, walked down certain streets and not others, then Sandra would come back to him. Nights terrified him, because he knew in advance that he would lie awake for hours, reliving those last hours with Sandra, again and again and again.

When he arrived home, there was a pile of post waiting for him. Among the advertising material and the bills there was a letter to Sandra. He saw that it was from a bookshop in the city and although he had never before opened his wife's post he felt that in the circumstances he had no choice.

The letter was reminding Sandra that the book she had ordered, *Virtual Reality and Abstract Truth*, was still waiting for her. Greg had not known that she had ordered the book, but he knew at once that she must have done it as a surprise for him. He was extremely moved, and he decided that the only thing he could do was to fetch it.

***

Although no one expected him to return to work, Greg felt that he would go completely mad if he did not have something else on which he could concentrate. Sitting at home day in and day out was not going to help him find Sandra, nor was it going to help him come to terms with the fact that she might never be found. He had, therefore, returned to work with the proviso that if necessary he could take more time off.

The bookshop was not far from his office, and he was able to walk there during his lunch hour. The young woman who dispensed orders was pleasant. She had actually read the book some weeks back, and she warmly recommended it.

'Definitely worth reading; gives you lots to think about,' she said as she returned Greg's credit card.

Greg took the book in its red and white plastic bag and walked out of the shop. Near the entrance he saw a tall middle-aged man with a large suitcase, the type with wheels and a retractable handle. The man was standing to the right of the entrance against the shop window. He had his back to the window and appeared to be watching the people passing him on the street. He did not look as though he had any intention of going into the shop; in fact, he did not look as though he had any intention of doing anything beyond standing where he was.

There was something about the man that vaguely interested Greg. He was well dressed, but somehow he seemed out of place, standing there with his large suitcase. Was he on his way to the airport, or had he come from the airport? There were no stickers on the suitcase, or not as far as Greg could see, but that did not necessarily mean anything. In this sophisticated age of e-tickets perhaps there were also e-stickers; not that it was really any of Greg's business.

Greg was about to walk past the man when the man pulled up the retractable handle on his maroon suitcase and said softly, 'Excuse me, but I believe I recognize you.'

Greg stopped and looked around him, wondering whether he had heard correctly, wondering whether the man was actually talking to him.

The man's hand was on the handle, and he looked as though he was about to move off, away from the book-shop window. 'From the newspapers,' he added.

Greg nodded. He had almost forgotten that his and Sandra's photos had been in all the newspapers and on the television.

'I recognized your wife as well,' he continued.

Greg looked surprised.

'I saw her once.' The man balanced the suitcase on its wheels, and he looked at Greg. 'I have a theory: I think I might know what happened to her,' he said. 'It's not that difficult actually; it's simply a matter of understanding the connections.'

6

Doug could not let go of the idea that he had somehow been responsible for Sandra's disappearance. When he was thinking logically he knew that the idea was quite ridiculous, but he argued with himself that had he told Greg about *all* the disappearances there was a chance that Greg and Sandra would never have gone to the track. And, if they had never gone there, then Sandra would doubtlessly not have disappeared.

He desperately needed to make amends, but he did not know how to go about it. The only way he could really atone for what had happened would be by finding Sandra, and given the number of people who had been unsuccessfully searching for her that seemed to be highly unlikely, if not impossible. In his free time, he would sometimes drive out to Shane's track and sit in his car, thinking. Yellow police tape had been strung across the entrance to the track in the hope that it might prevent people from going any further. The barrier, however, was not in any way solid, and there were a number of young people who took a delight in tempting fate by goading each other to cross it and then see how far they dared run along the track. Doug could understand the adrenalin rush they must have felt as they looked towards an unspecified danger that lacked definition: it was something that he might have done when he was younger. As he sat in his car, he sensed that although the danger was not obvious it was all around him like some kind of intangible mist. But he was not thinking about the danger, he was thinking that all he wanted was to be able to find Sandra and return her to Greg.

Initially, Doug had believed that Shane's disappearance was most probably linked to an unpaid debt. He had nothing concrete on which he could base such a belief, but of all the possibilities he felt that Shane's owing someone money was the most likely scenario. However, if Shane had disappeared because of a money problem, why then had so many others simply evaporated without trace? It was extremely unlikely that everyone owed the same person money. As the months and the years had passed, and more people vanished, Doug had been forced to revise his theory. By the time Sandra disappeared, Doug really had no idea why it was happening, but he did know that he was somehow to blame for the most recent disappearance.

Brian and Evans tried to talk to him, but their efforts lacked any real conviction. They had been with him at the pub that night, and even if Evans was fairly new to the district, Brian knew enough to have been able to fill Greg in on all those details that Doug had omitted. If Doug was at fault then they were also at fault. It was easiest to believe that none of them were at fault.

***

The Emergency volunteers, the police and the bushwalkers had failed to find any trace of Sandra, and after three weeks of intensive searching they were forced to admit that she was nowhere to be found. If she had not accidentally fallen or been murdered, and the body had then been completely vaporized, she must have been spirited away, but how or why no one had any idea. Several of the more energetic bushwalkers continued to do occasional searches, based mainly on unexplained spurts of intuition, but even they were eventually forced to give up. The police accepted that the investigation had hit a brick wall - there was no body, no clues, nothing - and although the case was still marked open it could no longer attract the same amount of attention and manpower.

Detective Senior Constable Dave Bennett, who had interviewed Greg on the day Sandra disappeared, was given the case files and put in charge of following up any new leads. Sitting in his small office that overlooked the town park, he had already decided that Sandra, like the four people before her, would most probably never be found.

Doug, on the other hand, sitting in his car near Shane's track, knew that there had to be an explanation for the disappearances. If he could work out *why* the five people had disappeared, then perhaps he could even work out where they were now.

Late one afternoon, several weeks after Sandra's disappearance, Doug drove out to Shane's track, but instead of remaining in the car, as he usually did, he got out of the car, stepped over the tape and started walking. He was becoming more and more certain that the track must have had something to do with all the disappearances, and he was sure that some piece of crucial evidence had been missed.

He walked slowly, looking at the vegetation on each side of the track and at the track itself, even though hundreds of footsteps had passed that way since Sandra had gone missing. He had absolutely no idea what it was that he was looking for, but he was strangely confident that whatever it was he would recognize it when, and if, he saw it.

Whether he was looking in all the wrong places or whether there was simply nothing to find, the track refused to reveal any of its secrets, and Doug soon found himself on the ridge without having seen anything that might confirm his theory. He was very familiar with the ridge: it was a place he often visited, especially when he needed to be able to get away from everything and, as he put it, chill out.

There was a breeze blowing in from the south-east, and the small white clouds from earlier in the afternoon had begun to join together, with an ominous greyness seeping into the white. After a few seconds of deliberation, Doug decided to ignore the changes to the weather, and he continued along the top of the ridge, wondering just how far Shane and the others had actually walked. It was common knowledge that Sandra had reached the ridge, as was the fact that she had then taken the track down towards the flat, but there had been nothing that indicated whether the other four had followed the same route or not. The main track ran along the ridge, and it made sense to Doug that anyone walking along the track would continue out along the ridge.

However, it was not long before the breeze became much stronger and seemed to be developing into something that resembled a minor gale. Doug looked at the sky, trying to remember if he had heard anything about a storm warning. He could see no point in walking any further along the ridge if the weather was going to get worse. His aim had been to reach the end of the ridge, about two kilometres further on, but another glance at the darkening sky made him turn around and begin to retrace his steps. Still thinking about the track and the route the other four may have taken, he felt that it possibly made more sense to assume that the others, like Sandra, had reached the ridge and had then followed the track downwards; yet, even while the thought was filling his head, it was being superseded by a new thought: why would Betsy Riley have walked all the way out to the ridge if her car had broken down on the other side of the road? While he was still trying to find an answer, an image of a German backpack pushed between rocks at the top of the ridge sidled across his mind, and he decided that it was not at all certain that all five people had continued beyond the ridge, or that they had even reached the ridge.

Walking back along the ridge, he had just reached the point where the track began to wind down to the open space below, when the rain started to fall. The sky was now quite dark, and the wind was becoming alarmingly wild. Doug made a quick decision: there was no way he would be able to return to his car before the storm hit; he would try to reach the hut further down the side of the ridge instead.

The hut had been built by a loner – Gordon, or some other name beginning with *G* – sometime in the 1920s or 1930s. He had worked on one of the properties further down on the plain, but then something had happened – no one seemed to know exactly what – and he had consequently disappeared. According to the rumours, Gordon was somehow involved in whatever it was that happened, but time had managed to erase all the facts, and Doug had to rely on a lot of opinions based only on hearsay. A year or so after Gordon had disappeared, someone caught sight of him on the ridge, and it did not take long before it became common knowledge that the man who had disappeared was living halfway up the ridge. Although he was no longer considered missing, Gordon was left alone, and it was assumed that he survived by killing the occasional rabbit and growing a few basic vegetables. In later years, the story had, however, evolved to the point where most people believed that Gordon's ex-employer left food and, at times, the odd piece of clothing at the hut, but by then it was no longer possible to know what was fact and what was merely gossip.

Gordon lived in the hut for a number of years and then moved on, leaving the hut to fend for itself. Years became decades. The occasional walker used the hut for shelter, but most of the time it was empty, a haven for birds and mice.

Doug manoeuvred his way down the fairly steep track. The sky above him was now quite threatening, and the rain had begun to fall in earnest. The back of the hut, with its gaping window, looked up towards the track, which passed around the side of the hut before continuing past the door and down the ridge.

By the time Doug reached the hut, he could barely see where he was going for the rain, and he was wet through. He pushed open the door and thankfully fell inside, pulling the door closed behind him. It was relatively dark inside, and some rain was coming in through the open window, but it was a good deal better than being outside. He ran his hands through his wet hair and tried, rather unsuccessfully, to brush the water off his shirt and trousers. Then he lowered himself to the floor next to the door and leant against the wall. There was not much else he could do; he would have to remain where he was until the storm passed.

With the rain resembling a heavy, opaque drape, he could barely see the track through the open window in front of him, but what he could or could not see was not really of any importance: he was simply grateful that he had been able to find shelter, no matter how primitive. The only piece of furniture remaining in the hut was a roughly constructed bench that had been pushed up against the back wall under the open window. Doug could not see the top of the bench from where he was sitting on the ground, but he guessed that it was probably like the rest of the hut: dirty and covered with bird and animal droppings. With the amount of rain coming in through the window, he also guessed that it was very wet.

His eyes fell on the fireplace, and he tried to imagine what it would be like with a blazing fire. It would at least have given him a chance to dry himself. He first assumed that the fireplace had not been used for ages, but when he stood up and moved closer he could see a small pile of grey ash and a half-burnt log. As he absent-mindedly began stirring in the ash with a twig that he found lying on the floor of the hut, he noticed something else. A small piece of burgundy-coloured paper or cardboard. He picked it out of the ash and took it to the open window to have a better look. It was roughly about four or five centimetres square, and the edges had been badly singed. He tried to work out what it might have been, and while he felt that it was probably not at all important he was also trying to think creatively. He hesitated for a moment, and then he slipped it into his wallet.

The rain was still battering against the roof, and there were gusts of water coming in through the window.

He was about to move away from the window when he looked up and, through the heavy veil of rain, he could make out the figure of a man in a grey-green raincoat walking down the track towards the hut.

Doug looked around him. There was absolutely nowhere to hide, and he had a sinking feeling that the man in the raincoat was not someone he really wanted to meet. If he had been able to vanish into thin air he would have done so willingly, but unfortunately he had never learnt the technique. The man was coming closer, and Doug had still not worked out an escape plan. All he could do was to hope that the man would continue past the hut and down the ridge, but something was telling him that that was not likely to happen.

7

'Connections? What on earth do you mean?' Greg could still remember how bewildered he had been. There were so many questions he needed to ask, but the man with the suitcase had already moved into the middle of the footpath and was walking away from him.

Greg had hurried after him, bumping into pedestrians, apologizing, focused only on the word *connections*.

He caught up to him further along the street and asked in a voice louder than he had intended, 'What do you mean by connections? 'What kind of connections?'

The man looked at Greg for a moment before replying, 'Everything is connected. Nothing can exist without being in a relationship to something or someone else.'

Greg was confused. He said, 'That may be so, but how will it help me get Sandra back?' He was not only confused, he was also extremely irritated. He disliked the way the man with the suitcase kept walking, in spite of all the people pushing around them. He would have stopped following him, but he needed to understand what the man was talking about.

The man stopped at the side of the footpath. He seemed oblivious of everyone else on the street. He said, 'When something happens, there are always strings stretching out in different directions, all of them connected to an infinity of different situations, happenings and people. Follow the strings from the happening at the centre, and you will see the connections; you may even understand why whatever it was that happened actually happened.'

Greg was about to say something, but the man was still speaking.

'We are so used to isolating parts, we often miss the whole. Everything is part of the whole; everything is connected. Look for the connections.'

Before Greg could reply, the man had tipped his suitcase on to its wheels and had disappeared into the crowd.

***

Back home, Greg was still feeling unsettled and irritated. It was most likely that the man was eccentric, even crazy. Greg could understand that it would have been easy for the man to recognize him, and even Sandra, from the photos of them in the media, yet what he had said about strings and connections was quite insane. Greg was annoyed that he had allowed himself be drawn in to such an extent, to the point where he had actually chased the man down the street.

When he phoned his sister, she agreed with him: the man was definitely a crackpot.

But, when the confusion and irritation and annoyance had abated, Greg found that he could not let go of the idea the man had placed in his head: the possibility that by following strings he might be able to find his wife. Imagine if the man was not mad; imagine if he was actually right. The man *seemed* quite normal: he had obviously given some thought to what he was wearing, and he looked intelligent, but perhaps the way one looked or dressed had little or no bearing on one's sanity. Greg was really not sure. He wondered what Sandra's disappearance might have been connected to. The other people who had disappeared? The town? Someone in a restaurant where they ate? Even the man with the suitcase?

In his head, he listed the names of the five missing people and then mentally checked through a number of different categories: age, sex, nationality, civil status, religion, employment...

Two women and three men; two in their twenties, two in their thirties and one over sixty; one married, one divorced, one widowed and two bachelors (though he was not completely sure that they *were* bachelors; they could have both been married or even divorced for all he knew). He was not too sure about religion, but from what he had picked up over the past weeks, he guessed that there were at least two Protestants and one Catholic. Nationality was somewhat easier: three Australians and two Germans.

Greg shut his eyes and wondered where he was supposed to find the connection; he also wondered if he was possibly losing the plot. Part of him insisted that he should ignore the man's suggestion completely, but there was a small part that kept saying: 'What if...' When he listened to that small part, as he was doing at the moment, he was sure that the connection or connections had to include all five people. Perhaps the connection was simply that they were all people, or perhaps the connection was something else entirely.

Of course the connection at the very centre was the fact that they were all missing, but that was obvious. That was why he was trying to find answers. If he followed that fact along the five strings stretching out from the centre, he arrived at what he imagined were five very different people. What he was looking for were the strings joining these people, a bit like the threads in a spider's web, but perhaps he had completely misunderstood; perhaps there were no such connections.

Greg decided that it was a futile endeavour. It was not unlike walking along a pitch black tunnel where smaller tunnels branched off at unexpected distances. He had absolutely no idea of where he was going or of where he was likely to end up. If he was walking through a system of dark tunnels then what he probably needed was a torch.

If there was the remotest possibility of success, Greg knew that he had to find that torch.

His copy of *Virtual Reality and Abstract Truth* was lying on the table, and the cover, black with red and white lettering, was grabbing for his attention. While he was still thinking about connections and torches, he began to think about the words *virtual reality*. It was an expression that he had heard a lot, especially in relation to computer games. In that context, there was a definite feeling of *unreality* lurking behind the word *reality*. As far as Greg understood, virtual reality meant essential existence – it was probably not possible to get anything more real than essential existence. On the other hand, he felt that there may be a conflict between the two words *abstract* and *truth*: could something be abstract or unreal and, at the same time, both truthful and accurate? He would have to give it some thought.

He opened the book. He had read the introduction on his train trip home from the city, and he was certain that the book was going to be interesting. The author seemed to share a number of his own ideas and theories, but the fact that it had been Sandra who had wanted to buy it for him meant that she was somehow present, looking over his shoulder. He could hear her voice, smell her perfume, see the way she moved...

He gave up trying to read and sat, looking out of the window in front of him. It was late afternoon, and the sun was beginning to set. The colours moving across the sky made him think of how the whole dreadful saga had begun: a chain of seemingly unconnected situations, which were in fact connected.

There was that word again. *Connection*.

He thought back over his list of missing people. Perhaps he was ignoring something? Perhaps there *was* a connection there somewhere, linking all five people, and he was simply too dense to see it.

Greg stood up and walked into the lounge room. He turned on the television, but there did not seem to be anything worth watching, so he turned it off again. He pulled off his shoes and lay on the couch, his arms behind his head, his eyes fixed on the ceiling. He knew that he had to think outside of the square; he needed to think both horizontally and vertically at the one and same time. His mind moved around the names and the different headings he had set up in his head.

Civil status. The possibilities were both elective and non-elective. Not everyone would choose to be widowed; in fact, the more he thought about it, the same could be said about divorced and married. Civil status was flexible, changeable, and yet, at the same time, it was like an anchor in society; it affected everyone, no one could avoid it. Even the hermit, living an isolated life in the bush, was single or divorced or...

Greg thought about the other headings. Perhaps gender and nationality could also be said to be elective and non-elective, but he was not quite sure if they fitted in with his theory quite as well as civil status. Admittedly some people changed their gender, but it could be argued that they were simply assuming what was their birthright. Nationality was more difficult: some people had three different nationalities, all of them at the same time. Greg decided that it would be a bit difficult to be both single and married - or single, married and divorced - at the exact same time.

His mind swung back to civil status. Was that where he would find the connection? Shane was divorced and Betsy Riley was widowed. What was it that connected these two people?

His eyes had picked up a small mark on the ceiling, and he wondered what it reminded him of. After a few minutes of wondering, he decided that it resembled an amoeba. He remembered learning about amoebae when he was at school. Single cells with the ability to change shape, similar to a person changing his or her civil status. The person remained basically the same, but the way he or she was perceived externally was different. A single amoeba or a widowed amoeba.

Loss.

The word rushed at him, pushing past all his other thoughts. Both Shane and Betsy had experienced loss; one was, in all probability, a voluntary decision, the other happened without consultation. In both cases, the people with whom Shane and Betsy had shared their lives had moved on.

Greg was not sure if he was on the right path. He had no idea about the two German boys: were they engaged, single, married? When he thought of Sandra, he suspected that he could not possibly be on the right path: she was happily married. Loss was not part of the equation. But, try as he might, he could not rid himself of the thought.

He slept badly that night, and by morning he had made a decision: he would ask for time off work and return to the country town. The man's suggestion seemed ludicrous, but Greg felt that he had to check it out to the best of his ability. Whatever the connections were that he had been talking about, Greg knew that if he ignored them, even if he had no idea what he was looking for, he would continue to speculate as to whether or not he had missed an opportunity to find Sandra.

***

Detective Senior Constable Dave Bennett was of the same opinion as Greg's sister: anyone talking about "connections" as a way of solving a crime would have to be completely mad. He was incredulous when Greg posed the question, and he felt that Greg must be more than a little strange to have taken it all so seriously. However, somewhere inside of him, Dave could understand that Greg was clutching at straws, and if one of these straws happened to have the word *connections* scrawled across it then so be it.

Dave felt genuinely sorry for Greg, but he was a very practical, down-to-earth person, and he steered clear of anything that even hinted of new age, alternative ideas. Looking for *connections* definitely fell into that category.

He shook his head and told Greg that he was still hoping that they would find Sandra, but it was now almost two months, and, although it upset him to say it, there was a chance that she would not be found. Not one of the other four had been found, and it was already more than five years since Shane Lachlan had disappeared, but if Sandra was to be found then it would be as the result of normal policing.

He looked at Greg thoughtfully for a moment and then sighed. 'I'm not at all interested in any kind of *connections*,' he said, 'but I'll go through all the files again. Perhaps there is something we missed; perhaps there is a common denominator that we have not noticed.'

Greg was not sure if he felt dejected or foolish or a mixture of both. At least he had given it a try. As he was leaving the office, he remembered Hans Neumann and Friedrich Keller. Although he knew that Dave would probably interpret the question as bordering on the absurd, he asked him if he knew anything about the relationship status of the missing German boys.

For a very long moment the detective said nothing.

Greg was uncomfortably aware that he had probably overstepped some invisible line of police etiquette. Or was it simply that fragile line between sane and insane?

The moment, like a still in the middle of a film, came to an end. Dave sighed, opened the drawer, pulled out the file on the two Germans and quickly leafed through to the relevant pages. Hans had broken up with his girlfriend of two years a couple of months before the pair left Germany to travel to Australia, while Friedrich's fiancée had been killed in a bus accident in Spain around the same time. The backpacking holiday to Australia had doubtlessly been an attempt for them both to come to terms with what had happened.

Greg's mind was ticking. Four of the missing people had experienced loss, but what about Sandra? Was it her loss or was it his?

Dave closed the folder and said, not at all unkindly, 'You need to be able to step back from all of this, Payne. Have you considered professional help? See a counsellor, take a holiday, try to move on with your life. Prepare yourself for the possibility that we may not be able to find Sandra, connections or no connections.'

8

The man walking down the track was coming closer to the hut, and Doug knew that he had to think of something very quickly. There was a chance that he was friendly – a walker, like himself, caught in the storm – but there was always a small chance that he was not at all friendly. Too many people had already disappeared, and Doug did not especially want to be added to the list. He looked around, an overwhelming sense of panic already spreading through his body. There was absolutely nowhere to hide: he was standing in an almost empty one-room building with a door facing the track and two windows…

An open window.

The man had already passed the back of the hut and, unless he were to suddenly diverge off the track into the bush, he would very soon be at the front. Without any time for careful, considered thought, Doug quickly pulled himself up on to the bench, not sure whether or not it would support his weight, and heaved himself through the open window. As his feet struck the sodden ground below, he heard the door of the hut open.

Crouched beneath the window, uncomfortably aware of the wetness all around him, he dared not move; he scarcely dared breathe, but he knew that he would have to find cover quickly: there was no guarantee that the man would not suddenly look out the window. Keeping close to the building, he crawled along the wall and around the side of the hut. Once he was away from the window and up against the side wall of the hut, where there was no window, he made a dash for a large outcrop of rock. It was still pouring rain, and he was thankful for the persistent noise that more than covered any sound he might have inadvertently made. Hidden behind the rocks, he waited to see if the man in the hut had possibly heard or seen anything. Minutes ticked by, but no one rushed out of the hut. As the adrenaline level in his body began to recede, he decided that he would have to return to the top the ridge by another route – as far as he was concerned, nothing could possibly persuade him to use the track.

***

It took Doug almost two hours to get back to his car. The climb up on to the ridge over slippery rocks and boulders and through thick, wet vegetation was something he was hoping would for ever remain a one-off experience. In parts the ground was perilous, and the rain did not let up, not even for a few minutes. By the time he had navigated the last few rocks and boulders and had pulled himself up on to the top of the ridge, he was both exhausted and completely drenched. There was, however, absolutely no point in stopping, and, having finally connected with the main track, he pushed on to the car.

When, some thirty minutes later, he reached the end of the track and unlocked his car, he had a new understanding of the word *grateful*. He was muddy, sopping wet and shaking all over, though whether this was from the saturation he had sustained or whether it was from pure fear he was not sure. He turned on the ignition, the windscreen wipers and the air conditioning. While he waited for the windscreen to clear, he thought through the events of the afternoon. He was still speculating as to whether he had been unnecessarily suspicious and whether there was a chance that the man was actually quite harmless. He was not sure what he had achieved, if anything, and he was certainly no closer to solving the mystery of Sandra's disappearance, but at least he had a small piece of something that could turn out to be evidence and which might help move the investigation in a more positive direction.

An elusive yet worrying thought was nudging at his mind, pulling at his memory; at its centre was the man with the raincoat. He had only seen him for a few seconds, and the conditions had been appalling, but now he had been left with this strange, clinging feeling.

He wondered if he had not seen him somewhere before.

***

The following day, Detective Senior Constable Dave Bennett was surprised by a visit from Doug. He had not spoken to him since the day Sandra had gone missing, and he was vaguely curious as to the purpose of the visit.

He looked at the fragment of card and listened while Doug related what had happened to him the previous day. Although Dave had his suspicions as regards the piece of card, he resisted the temptation to put any kind of equals sign between the card, the man in the raincoat and the missing people. However, the possibility that he may have overlooked something during the initial investigation of the site worried Dave: he knew how vital those first couple of hours were. If he had missed one small piece of evidence, then it was possible that he had also missed something bigger, something that could have given him a clue as to what might have happened to Sandra.

The card fragment was sent to Canberra for forensic testing, and Dave waited impatiently for the results. When they finally came, a few days later, they were disappointing. The fragment did not belong to a German European passport. Dave had been hoping that his suspicions might have been correct, because then he would have received confirmation that the disappearances – at least those of Hans Neumann and Friedrich Keller – were not accidental. If a passport (or both passports) had been burnt then it would have shown that someone had wanted to dispose of evidence, and the fact that a second person, a perpetrator, was involved meant that Dave would have been looking for an actual person. In a small way, it may have made his job easier.

Dave slipped the forensic report and the piece of card into the drawer with the folders of the five missing people. Even though the card fragment had been shown not to be pertinent to the investigation, he felt that it still warranted a place in the drawer.

He could not shake the feeling that he may have overlooked something else, and his thoughts now moved to the man in the raincoat. He sent out a new investigation team with orders to check every square centimetre of the hut. Although several different sets of fingerprints were found and boot prints were taken from the earthen floor, there was nothing that indicated who the man might have been and definitely nothing that gave any lead as to why he had visited the hut.

As far as Dave was concerned, everything would be

much easier if it could be proved that there was an outside person involved in all the disappearances; in fact he was convinced that this was the case. It was just a matter of finding him or her. He did not feel that the disappearances were necessarily caused by people falling off the edge of cliffs or getting hopelessly lost; if that were the case he felt that, by this stage, they should have found at least one body, if not more.

***

Like Shane, Doug was divorced. He had managed four years of marriage, but then the relationship had collapsed, and Cheryl had moved to Sydney with their three-year-old daughter. Doug had lamely objected to his ex-wife and daughter moving so far away, but Cheryl insisted that there were more opportunities in Sydney, especially now she was on her own. Well, not exactly on her own, there was the new boyfriend and, of course, Kylie. That was ten years ago, and during this time Kylie's visits to her father had become less and less frequent: Doug was now lucky if he saw his daughter twice a year.

The incident at the hut had shaken him more than he first thought, and after a couple of weeks of attempting to come to terms with what he had done and what he should have done he decided that he needed to have a break away from the town. The uncomfortable feeling that the man in the raincoat may have been someone he had seen before would not leave him. He phoned Greg and asked if there was a possibility he could put him up the following weekend: he would catch up with Kylie, and hopefully there would be some time over when he and Greg could talk through a few things that he had on his mind.

He arrived late on the Friday evening, and on the Saturday he took Kylie to Darling Harbour. They visited the Aquarium, strolled around the Maritime Museum, caught a show at the Imax theatre and ate fast food at two different places. By the time he had returned Kylie to her mother and stepfather, it was after eight in the evening and almost nine before he reached Greg's place.

***

Greg had not heard about Doug's experience at the hut, and he tried to keep his imagination from running away with him while Doug told him what had happened out on the ridge. Even though the image of a man in a raincoat, walking along the ridge in a wild storm, could be pushed and pulled in different directions until it fitted in with his theory that Sandra may have been kidnapped (Greg had several theories as to what might have happened to his wife), he had to admit to himself that there was nothing obvious that tied the man to the disappearances. It was more than possible that the man, like Doug, had simply been seeking shelter from the storm. Yet, in the back of his head, Greg kept returning to the probability that someone else was involved and that the disappearances were not simply the result of accidents. He fetched another couple of beers from the fridge and then, suddenly changing the conversation, he told Doug that he was seeing a counsellor.

Dave's parting words a few weeks earlier, had had a marked effect on Greg. For the first time since that awful day in January, Greg had been forced to look at himself through someone else's eyes. That he had been able to be swayed by a stranger in the street told him that he definitely needed to get a hold on himself.

'A counsellor?' repeated Doug. There was a touch of something new in his voice; Greg was not sure if it was incredulity or sympathy.

Greg shrugged. He did not know Doug very well: they were simply colleagues who met occasionally. He had no intention of telling him about the man who had talked about following threads and looking for connections. Nor did he want to talk about Dave Bennett's reaction when he mentioned the word to him. It had been Dave's reaction that had made him reassess everything and contact a grief counsellor. He had already had three sessions with him, and he knew that it had been the right decision. He had been so sure that he would be able to get through it all on his own, but now he knew otherwise.

'It's been a difficult few months,' Greg said, looking at Doug. He pushed one of the beers towards Doug and opened the other one for himself. 'I guess I simply reached a point where I knew I needed help.'

Doug took the beer and nodded his thanks. He gave no indication as to what he was thinking; instead he apologized, yet again, for not having given Greg the whole story.

Greg shook his head. He blamed himself, not Doug, and he found Doug's need to apologize strangely confronting: it reminded him too much of what he should never have done. He moved away from such thoughts, and he talked about the counsellor. 'He's helped me see things in perspective,' Greg said, putting the empty can on the table, 'the pain, the anger and the dreadful sense of loss are all still there, but perhaps I'll eventually be able to move outside of such feelings, beyond them. Not yet, but eventually... '

Doug nodded again. Perhaps he was also thinking of things that he needed to be able to move beyond.

'I mean,' said Greg, looking at his hands, 'Sandra might not be coming back. Perhaps they will never find her... it's already three months, and there's been no sign, no clue. Nothing. I have to go on living, even if... '

Doug finished the sentence for him. '... she doesn't come back.'

No one said anything for a few moments, then Doug said, 'I've been thinking a lot... about the track. After all, no matter how you look at it, it's the track that's the common factor.'

Although Greg asked, 'Common factor?' He knew exactly what Doug was saying. The thought had been there, in the back of his mind, all along. The one thing that was common to each disappearance was the track. Perhaps it was the track that was the *connection* the man was talking about?

'You know, the red thread... or whatever. They all went missing on that track.'

Greg nodded slowly. Was it just the track that was the connection, or was there something else as well? Was he right when he guessed that *loss* was a connection? Was there one main connection and lots of sub-connections, or did all the connections come together in some way to form that aha moment?

Greg could feel himself slipping back into his old way of thinking, his way of thinking before he met the counsellor. He knew that he needed to take hold of himself. Thinking about connections was not going to help him find Sandra, nor was it going to help him return to a normal, balanced life.

He agreed with Doug about the track, and then, although he felt that Doug may have wanted to say something else about the track, he changed the subject and they talked about the office, the town and, finally, Doug and Kylie's outing in Sydney.

Late the following morning when Greg was organizing himself to drive Doug to the airport, he noticed that he had missed a call on his phone. When he checked it, he saw that it was from Dave. When Dave had been unable to contact Greg – his phone had been lying on the desk in his office all evening – he had left a text message: *Human remains found below hut. As yet unidentified. Will contact you on Monday.*

Greg's first impulse was to book himself on to the same plane as Doug and get to the town as quickly as possible: he could be at the police station by mid-afternoon. However, the more he thought about it the more he realized that there would be no point. Such forensic examination could take days, even weeks, and what would he do in the meantime? There was nothing at all in Dave's message that indicated that the remains belonged to Sandra. No matter what the counsellor was saying, it was important that he kept believing that she was still alive.

9

Greg was right in assuming that the forensic examination would take time. After two weeks of not hearing anything from Dave, he finally decided to visit the town again, wanting to believe that his physical presence might actually hurry things along. But the evening before he was due to travel, Dave phoned, apologized for the long delay and told him that the remains were not Sandra's; in fact, they did not belong to any of the missing persons. In a strange way, Greg found Dave's words consoling: they were like a waterfall of relief sweeping over his entire body. If the remains were not Sandra's, then there was a chance that she was still alive. She *was* still alive. He would not let himself believe otherwise.

He decided that he would still go ahead as planned and travel to the town. He had not been there since he had spoken with Dave about connections, and since then he had had several sessions with the counsellor. He needed to see if he could return to the town without being overwhelmed by all the assorted feelings of guilt, regret and loss.

Greg took his flight the following day, arriving mid-morning. After getting one of the very few taxis to the hotel where he usually stayed, he entered through the heavy timber door, with its large pane of blue, green and red stained glass, and walked to the check-in desk.

The receptionist was busy with another customer, and Greg whiled away a few minutes, looking at the pastoral scenes on the walls and the intricate pattern in the blue and grey carpet. Only when he became aware that the receptionist was almost finished with her customer did he direct his gaze to the other person standing at the desk.

The man standing barely metres from him was the man who had talked to him about connections.

Greg lowered his gaze, and, sure enough, there was the maroon suitcase.

The man, suddenly aware that Greg was looking at him, turned his head away from the receptionist and, after a brief moment of looking rather confused, said, 'Hello, Mr Payne. I certainly hadn't expected to see you.'

Greg did not know what to say, but he could very easily have said much the same thing.

'How are you going with the connections?' the man, who had now regained his composure, asked, while smiling at the receptionist and taking back his credit card.

Greg felt as though he were an actor in some kind of strange dream. 'It's not been easy,' he said, 'there are so many different kind of connections. I'm not quite sure... '

The man smiled again, this time directly at Greg. The smile completely interrupted what Greg was about to say.

The receptionist said, 'Thank you, Mr Tyler.'

Greg thought: *So he's called Tyler.*

Mr Tyler pulled up the handle on his suitcase. 'We will doubtlessly meet again, Mr Payne; it seems to be inevitable,' he said as he began to walk towards the entrance.

Greg, still somewhat dumbfounded, hesitated a moment and then said, 'Anything is possible... ,' but by the time he managed to speak Mr Tyler had already disappeared through the main door.

**

Greg was still musing about meeting up with the man with the suitcase, or Mr Tyler, when, a good half hour later, he walked into the police station. Dave Bennett was in the main office, discussing something with a colleague when Greg entered, and he seemed pleased to see him. After the initial greetings, Dave suggested that they move to his office. He then motioned Greg to a chair by the window, closed the door and sat down behind his desk.

'The remains... not exactly what we had expected but in many ways a relief. We really haven't come any further with the missing people,' he said, moving a few papers from one side of his desk to the other before shifting his gaze to Greg.

Greg leaned forward in his chair, 'But you did find out who the person was, or... ?'

Dave explained that the remains belonged to a man called Gordon Parrish. 'It's been a complicated business, finding out who he was. We didn't have a lot to go on; in fact we really had nothing.'

Greg was wondering if there could be anything that connected Gordon Parrish's death with the five missing people. Most of all he was thinking of Sandra. He really did not want there to be any kind of connection between Sandra and someone who had died, most probably in fairly tragic circumstances.

'It's a long story,' said Dave, looking at his watch, 'but

I can give you the abbreviated version.'

Greg nodded. The name Gordon Parrish meant nothing to him, but he was curious as to how the police had managed to connect a name with remains for which they had absolutely no information. Greg was also curious as to what Gordon Parrish had been doing on the ridge and how and, more importantly, when he had died.

'Gordon worked on one of the big farms below the ridge. He had a wife, I think her name may have been Anne or Anna, and they had a boy, Harold. In 1930, Harold was about four or five years old. The farm where Gordon worked was owned by MacPherson, a decent kind of fellow, but the farm manager, George, was another kettle of fish entirely: he was arrogant, violent and lazy. In a normal situation I suppose George would have been fired, but this was not what one would call a normal situation: George happened to be MacPherson's younger brother.'

Dave picked up a pen from the desk in front of him and rolled it around between his fingers.

'In the June of that year, Gordon arrived home after doing three days of fencing on the far side of the property to find Anna dead on the floor of the kitchen – she'd been stabbed a number of times – and the boy hiding in a cupboard in the hall. It was fairly clear that the murder had happened the same day that Gordon had returned home. Harold was far too traumatized to be interviewed, and it was very quickly assumed that Gordon was the perpetrator. As far as the police were concerned, there was no one else who could have done it.'

Dave pushed the pen away from him and continued, 'Gordon was taken into custody even though he vehemently declared that he had absolutely nothing to do with the murder and that the police should be out looking for the person who had so violently killed his wife.

'Anna's sister, Miriam, had always disliked Gordon intensely, and she was one of the few who vocally insisted that the police had found the right man. Miriam and her husband lived in the town, and with Anna dead and Gordon in gaol they stepped in as next of kin and took Harold. In some strange way, Miriam saw what had happened, tragic as it most definitely was, as a gift from God. Childless, Miriam was given an opportunity that was too good to refuse. Before a week had passed, Miriam and her husband had packed up and left the town, taking Harold with them. They left no forwarding address.

'Gordon believed he knew who had killed his wife, but no one was listening to him. MacPherson also had his suspicions, but for personal reasons he felt his hands were tied.

'Both of them suspected George.

Dave moved in his chair and picked up a pen lying on the desk in front of him. 'And with very good reason,' he said. 'From the information we've been able to unravel, George had pestered Anna on more than a couple of occasions, but she had completely ignored him. In all probability, she ignored him just once too often.'

Rolling the pen between his fingers, he said, 'From what I've heard, George was not the type of person who coped particularly well with being ignored.

'In the end, the police came to the conclusion that Gordon could not have done it. He had returned home well after the time frame for the murder established by the coroner. MacPherson agreed with them – he was certain that Gordon was innocent – but, while he vouched for Gordon's character, he was probably hoping that the investigation would die down and that no one would begin pointing the finger at George. It is most likely that he told his brother of his suspicions, because George left the property around this time, and he never returned.'

The phone rang. The noise was sharp and shrill, and both Dave and Greg, who were still caught up in the 1930s, jumped.

Dave apologized. 'I'll have to take this, I'm afraid.'

Greg left the room and closed the door quietly behind him. Out in the main office, he sat in one of the two chairs provided for visitors and picked up an out-of-date magazine. Eventually, Dave appeared, looking a little stressed, and Greg closed the magazine.

'Duty calls,' said Dave, 'but you'll be around for a day or so... ?'

Greg nodded. He was about to ask what happened to Gordon after he had been released, but a couple of police were already on their way towards the front door. Dave, one hand raised in parting, hurried to join them.

***

Greg left the police station, thinking about Tyler but also thinking about the man called Gordon. He wondered what had happened to him after he was released from gaol. Obviously he died, but when or how, Greg still had no idea.

He had nothing planned, and he was at a bit of a loss as to what to do for the rest of the day. Doug was at work, and although Greg knew that he could call in at the office he was reluctant to do so.

He could not remove Gordon from his head.

Then it suddenly occurred to him that the local newspaper would have been full of Gordon after the remains had been discovered. He needed to get hold of some

newspapers, or perhaps he could find what he was looking for online. He thought of his smartphone but decided
against it. There was a library a few blocks further down
the street; he would see if they had something.

As Greg had expected, the library had copies of the
local paper, and Greg began by looking at the paper that
was a week old, and then he worked his way towards
the most recent copy, thumbing through the pages,
looking for key words. In the paper from three days ago,
he found four pages devoted entirely to the discovery of
remains below the ridge, the police investigation and, of
course, Gordon. There were even photos.

Greg spread the paper out on the table in front of him
and began to read. Most of what Dave had told him was
in the paper, but there was much more, and it was what
Dave had not told him that interested Greg most.

He had already gathered that when Gordon was
finally released from gaol he must have discovered that
not only had he lost his wife he had also lost his son. No
one knew where Miriam, her husband and Harold had
gone. A handful of people were aware that the couple
had left the town with the boy, but no one was completely sure where they had been headed. Several
mentioned Sydney, and one person said he had a feeling
that they may have moved to Queensland, but as there
was no forwarding address Miriam, her husband and
Harold had literally and virtually vanished.

The police contacted their colleagues in Sydney and
Brisbane, electoral rolls were checked and a few possible
sightings were followed up, but it was as though Miriam
and her family had never existed. While the police were
fumbling around trying to find his son, Gordon handed
in his notice to MacPherson, and then he also disappeared.
The police decided that they had no reason to continue

the hunt for Harold, because even if they found him they could now no longer return him to his father, and the case was subsequently shelved.

It was assumed that Gordon was probably looking for his son, but a year or so later, he was discovered living in a hut halfway up the ridge. From things he later let slip to MacPherson, he had spent eight months searching the streets of Sydney and Brisbane, but he had not been overly confident that he would find Harold: he had no idea where he should be looking. The police, with all their contacts and resources, had failed dismally, so there was no reason why *he* should be successful. Eventually he returned to the town and built himself the hut below the ridge. He was angry, his heart was broken and he wanted nothing more to do with people. By the time he was discovered, he had become a recluse, and the towns- people, respecting his need to be on his own, let him be.

Even before Gordon returned to the ridge, the police had decided that George was a more likely suspect for the murder, but like Miriam and her husband he was nowhere to be found. They considered holding Mac- Pherson, believing that he knew where his brother was, but it very soon became evident that this was not so, and they had to admit that they had bungled the whole case right from the very beginning.

Greg reread a paragraph and then skipped a para- graph about police procedure in the 1930s. He looked at the photos, wondering all the time how and why Gordon had died and why it had taken so long for anyone to find his remains. The article went on to relate how, after several years, MacPherson had noticed that the hut was empty, and it was concluded that Gordon had finally left the district.

Almost seventy-five years later, a man hunting rabbits

along the top of the ridge missed his footing and fell into a shallow depression beneath an overhang of large rocks. He was shaken but unhurt. As he scrambled to his feet, his hand came in contact with something under a thin layer of leaves. Curious, he pushed aside the mulch and discovered something that looked very much like a human humerus.

It took the police investigation team quite some time to retrieve all the remains, many of them buried under at least a half metre of rock and sand. It was concluded that the man had fallen, or been pushed, into the depression, which several decades ago was probably much deeper. Over the years the depression had filled with debris from the surrounding vegetation - there could even have been a small landslide - and the body had completely disappeared. That one bone just happened to be lying so close to the surface was probably the result of animal activity.

The forensic investigation revealed that it was more than likely that the man had been stabbed.

Something was worrying Greg. He turned back to the previous page and skimmed what he had already read. It was something to do with Miriam and her husband, Bruce.

Then suddenly it was in front of him in black and white: Miriam and Bruce's surname was Tyler.

10

Doug had also read all the newspaper articles on the gruesome find up on the ridge; he had even googled 'remains' and the name of the town, and he had found a whole lot more connected and unconnected information, much of which he could probably have done without. What he had learnt simply underlined the feeling that he had had all along, the feeling that there was something strange, almost evil, hanging over the track and the ridge area. Unlike Greg, he had grown up hearing rumours about Gordon, and he had known part of his story, but he had not expected to discover that Gordon had met such a violent end. He kept thinking back to the hut, reflecting on the fact that both he and Gordon had stood in the same space, admittedly many, many years apart, and looked out on much the same scenery. His hands had touched the door, the bench and the fireplace... places where, undoubtedly, Gordon's hands would also have rested all those years earlier.

The image of both Gordon and himself sharing a space decades apart was shattered by the memory of the storm and the man on the track, a man he felt he may have recognized. After he had shared the incident with Greg on his recent trip to Sydney, Greg had told him about his own experience all those weeks ago, an experience, which, until then, he had evidently not shared with anyone. Doug remembered reliving his own moment of horror, watching the man approaching the hut, as Greg talked about how he had wanted to take a photo of the sunset and how he had ended up being trapped on the ridge all night, terrified that the two men, smoking only metres from where he was hidden, may have been looking for him. Doug could appreciate Greg's fear, especially when Greg mentioned the cigarette butts near his car.

He stood up from where he had been sitting in front of the computer and walked to the kitchen. He drank some water straight from the tap, deciding that everything to do with the track, plus the unexpected discovery of Gordon, was having too much of a negative effect on him. There was nothing to say that the man in the raincoat, or even the men smoking out on the ridge, meant any harm. As for Gordon, living for years in a hut before being murdered by some unknown person, it was definitely tragic, but it hardly had anything to do with him. It was clearly time to start thinking about other things.

While he was trying to forget the track and Gordon, there was one thought that refused to go away: *who was the man in the raincoat, and where had he seen him before?*

***

Back in Sydney in the seclusion of his own lounge room, a whisky in his hand, Greg was thinking over the events of the past few days. He had hoped to catch up with Dave Bennett the day after he had spoken with him at the police station, but the detective was in Canberra and was not expected back until late afternoon. Greg was already booked to return to Sydney on the afternoon flight. He had briefly considered changing his booking to the following day, but he finally decided that Dave had probably told him most of what he needed to know, and he could always phone him if he had further questions.

When he realized that he would not be catching up with Dave, he wandered across to the library and borrowed one of the public computers. He was still trying to absorb the fact that the man with the suitcase was actually called Tyler and that he was, in some strange way, connected with the town, the ridge, Gordon and perhaps even the missing people. It was even conceivable that he actually *did* know something about Sandra. Greg's thoughts went back to what Tyler had said to him about connections all those weeks ago; perhaps he should have been listening more closely. He was beginning to suspect that he should have done as Tyler suggested: perhaps he should have continued to look for connections.

He typed in *Tyler*, hoping that something might come up that would shed a light on *his* Mr Tyler. It was obvious that the man had to be connected to the couple who had abducted Harold. He could hardly be Harold, but he could be Harold's son.

There were thousands of search results. He glanced through the first couple of pages where most of the entries had *Tyler* as a given name, and then he typed in Bruce Tyler. He found a Bruce J. Tyler, a barrister in New York, and another Bruce Tyler, an artist from Edinburgh. There was no mention of Bruce Tyler from Sydney. Of course, it had been a long shot, and both Bruce and Miriam would have died years ago, well and truly before online-information collection and google searches. He did not know Tyler's given name, so he had to admit that he had hit a brick wall. Disappointed, he logged out of the computer and left the library.

Now, sitting in his lounge room, Greg noticed with the slightest sensation of surprise that his glass was already empty. He stood up and took the glass with him to the other side of the room where the bottle was still standing on what he liked to call 'the bar'. Sandra used to roll her eyes at him when he mentioned 'the bar'; it was, after all, nothing more than a two-shelved, waist-high timber cupboard in a corner of the room, with a faux marble top. He poured himself some more whisky and returned the bottle to its place in the cupboard. With the glass in his hand, he walked across to the full-length French windows that looked out on to the garden.

His thoughts slipped back to the book he had been reading, *Virtual Reality and Abstract Truth*. He remembered a passage that stated that things are rarely the way we believe them to be and that much of the time reality is completely obscured by illusion; in fact illusion can sometimes be more accurate than our perception of reality. Greg wondered if there was an answer for him there somewhere. Perhaps he needed to let go of all the obvious facts and follow his intuition. It was even possible that he should be following some course of action that, on the surface at least, appeared unlikely to lead anywhere in particular.

For some reason, he could not get the word *connections* out of his head.

"*Our world, what we perceive around us as being real, is, on the one hand, essentially real for us in the moment of perception, and yet, at the same time, it can be completely unreal...* " What was it that he was perceiving as being real but which, for whatever reason, was not real at all? Was it the fact that he was standing at the window, looking out towards the garden, or was it something completely different? Perhaps it had something to do with Sandra. Perhaps she was not missing at all.

It was already May, and, as Greg looked out the window, he could see that there were autumn reds and yellows mixed with the eucalyptus evergreens and the very end of the dahlias. Sandra had planted the dahlias all those months ago, and now...

He forced his thoughts away from Sandra and his book and back to the town and what he had been doing there.

After the library, he had called around to the office. It was not because of any desire to meet up with his work colleagues but more because he felt that he probably owed it to Doug. Doug would doubtlessly think it rather strange if he were later to learn that Greg had been in the town and had failed to connect with him.

As it turned out, Doug was not in the office. Greg wrote a few lines on a sticky note, saying that they could hopefully meet up next time he was in the town, stuck it on Doug's computer, exchanged a couple of necessary pleasantries with the secretary and left the office.

Once more out the street, he was not sure what he should do next, when he noticed a woman on the other side of the street. She was probably in her mid or late sixties, short and fairly ordinary looking. There was something about her that puzzled Greg; he knew that he should not stare, but he had a feeling that he knew her. At the very least, he had seen her somewhere, but he could not remember where.

The woman obviously felt the same about him, because she crossed the road and came up to him, her hand outstretched.

'It's Mr Paynter, isn't it?' she said as she took his hand.

'Payne,' said Greg, 'Greg Payne. And you're... ?'

'Oh, I'm so sorry. Thelma,' she said. 'You probably don't remember me; I'm Betsy's sister.'

Now Greg remembered. They had all been at a meeting Dave Bennett had organized months ago, not long after Sandra had disappeared. Dave had hoped that having everyone together in the same room might have helped jolt people's memories or, at the very least, bring new information to the surface. It had not worked.

Greg knew that he should have recognized Thelma; he felt annoyed with himself that he had not.

Thelma was talking again, asking him how he was managing, regretting the fact that it had been so long and that there was still no news. While she talked, she reached out and touched his arm.

The small gesture of kindness was unexpected, but Greg did not back away from it. He nodded and said that he was going along as well as could be expected. Then he remembered Betsy and quickly added that Thelma probably understood only too well how he was feeling and where he was at.

He was constantly forgetting that there were other people feeling much the same as he was, people who went to bed every night, hoping that their loved one would be miraculously returned to them the following day.

Thelma said, 'Mr Payne, Greg... I should probably tell you. Something quite strange happened a few days ago. It might be a sign of sorts; I'm not sure. It's to do with Betsy.'

Greg's heart started to beat faster. The words: *It's to*

do with Betsy began to fill his mind until there was not much room left for anything else. Perhaps Thelma had seen her, or perhaps she had some other reason to believe that Betsy was still alive. If Betsy were alive then perhaps they were *all* alive.

With a mental jerk, he put the brakes on his train of thought and tried to clear his mind of what he was simply imagining. Thelma had not even said anything yet, and he was already letting his thoughts rush off on a tangent of their own. He realized only too well that he was hurtling into an area that had very little to do with reality and everything to do with wishful thinking. After all the hours with the counsellor, Greg was finally learning to edit some of his more wayward feelings: he was beginning to accept the difference between self-deception and reality. But sometimes it just did not work.

Thelma leaned closer to Greg as a large semi-trailer rumbled down the main street. In spite of the noise, Greg was still able to hear what she said.

What she told him was unbelievable. As he looked at her, completely lost for words, he wondered if perhaps there was something to be said for wishful thinking after all.

***

Greg phoned Dave the day after he returned to Sydney and learnt that his suspicions had been true: Gordon Parrish had been identified by cross-referencing DNA with a relative. It was a man from Sydney who had contacted the investigation team completely out of the blue. He told them that he was contacting them because he had seen something on the television about remains being found, and he had then added that he might be able to help them with the identification.

Dave had explained that the man was called Vincent Tyler, and it turned out that he was Gordon Parrish's grandson. He had known that his grandfather had lived on the ridge back in the 1930s and that he had disappeared sometime around 1940. It was just a matter of him putting two and two together.

'We were a bit hesitant at first,' Dave continued, 'but Tyler flew across from Sydney, and the forensic people came up from Canberra and took DNA samples. There was no question. The DNA was the same. The remains had to be Gordon Parrish.'

Greg found the story interesting, but he could not help but wonder what Dave would have said if he had told him that it was Vincent Tyler, the very same Vincent Tyler, who had talked to him about *connections*.

While he was thinking about Gordon and Vincent Tyler and connections, he was also thinking about what Thelma had told him. He desperately wanted to talk to Dave about it, but before he was able to frame the words into a sentence, Dave excused himself and said that he really had to go.

Greg sat there, the telephone still in his hand, remembering what Thelma had said to him.

'It's happened twice now,' she had said.

Greg remembered asking her what it was that had happened.

'She phoned me, but when I started to answer, she just hung up.'

'She... ?'

'Betsy,' she had said over the top of the noise.

When he finally regained the power of speech, he asked her, 'Have you mentioned this to Dave... Senior Constable Bennett?'

Thelma nodded. 'I did, and he did say that he'd look into it. He didn't sound convinced that it was Betsy who phoned; he said that there was a very good chance that the phone had been stolen and that it was someone else making the call.'

11

Vincent Tyler had been genuinely surprised to see Greg at the hotel. However, when he thought about it later, he could understood that it was not at all strange that Greg should have been in the town: the remains could have belonged to anyone, and it was more than possible that Greg did not know that they had already been identified. Had Vincent had more time, he might have considered talking with Greg, but he had a flight to catch, and he doubted that anything he might have said would have helped Greg. As far as he was concerned, nothing would help Greg as long as he was refusing to accept that it was important to be able to find the connections.

On the plane back to Sydney, he had had plenty of time to think back over the meeting with Detective Senior Constable Dave Bennett. Vincent's first impression of Dave was that he was an extremely ordinary man, in fact *ordinary* with a capital 'O'. He felt that the senior constable needed to loosen up a little and move out of his tunnel; he needed to be able to accept less conservative ways of problem solving. He was dealing with five missing people, and he definitely needed to be agile in his thinking. Vincent knew that the answer was hidden there somewhere; possibly behind something that no one had even considered. As he had already said to Greg, it was just a matter of seeing what connected with what.

Dave had been politely wary when Vincent presented himself at the station. Vincent sensed from the initial exchange of words and the nonchalant handshake that he was being summed up either as a potential crackpot or as the key-breaker in a rather difficult case. It had taken at least ten minutes before the detective chose the second of these two possibilities. He had obviously come to the conclusion that Vincent was actually sane and that he could very well have something sensible to relate.

Even before the forensic examination and the DNA testing, which conclusively proved his theory, Vincent believed that the remains belonged to Gordon Parrish, his grandfather. As he told Dave, the remains were the last link in a saga spanning almost a century.

Initially, Vincent was relieved to have finally discovered the end of Gordon's story; however, he was greatly disturbed to hear that his relative had been murdered. The fact that there was another person involved in his grandfather's death meant that Vincent had not reached the end at all. He felt that he needed to find out who had murdered Gordon and why, but the likelihood of that happening was probably nil: the perpetrator, and anyone who might have known anything about the murder, would have died years ago.

From what Dave Bennett told him, Vincent understood that the detective was not unfamiliar with the story of Gordon Parrish, that is to say, up until he disappeared. Dave also knew that Gordon's sister-in-law had taken Gordon's son and then, together with her husband, had managed to somehow slip off the planet. Vincent was more than happy to fill in all the gaps.

In late 1930 or early 1931, Miriam and Bruce arrived

in Sydney with Harold, who was naturally assumed to be their son. They settled in Balmain, a working-class suburb fringing a small section of the harbour, and Bruce was fortunate to be able to find work with a bread carter. Then, a year or so later, the Depression turned the country upside down, and Bruce found himself unemployed without any prospect of finding another job. After several months of joining dole queues, while wondering whether it might make more sense to return to the country, Bruce turned out to be one of the few lucky ones. After a tip-off from a friend, he found employment at the new Balmain Power Station, sorting garbage for the incinerator.

Then the war came and, in 1943, Harold, now eighteen, joined the army and was almost immediately shipped to New Guinea. Early in 1944, he was badly wounded at Sio and was evacuated to Darwin where he spent several weeks in a military hospital. He was eventually deemed unfit for further service, was given an honourable discharge and was returned to Sydney.

By this time, Bruce, still working at the Power Station, had risen to the level of foreman, and he managed to secure a position for Harold in the administration department. Harold had never expected to finish up in an office, but his leg was more or less useless for anything more physical. He was still using a crutch, and he had to accept that New Guinea would always be the dividing line between his past and future lives.

Harold was almost thirty-five before he married, and both Miriam and Bruce had given up hoping that it would ever happen. He had always been a shy person, and after his injury he became, if possible, even more withdrawn and distant. When Miriam looked at him, she could not but fail to see Gordon, and there were occasions when she experienced small twinges of conscience: perhaps in her impatience to secure the child she had always longed for she had completely lost sight of the big picture. Perhaps she had done something for which there could be no forgiveness, not here on earth and most definitely not in the afterlife. She knew that Gordon had been proven innocent and had been released from gaol; she also knew that he had later disappeared. She very occasionally wondered whether, and just how much, her actions were responsible for Gordon's withdrawal to a hut in the middle of the bush and, later, for his disappearing altogether.

Bruce had never been happy about what they had done or about the move to the city: he was a country boy, and he disliked the noise and bustle of the city. But after marrying Miriam he very soon learnt that Miriam's will was paramount, and if there were to be any form of peace in the marital home it was essential that she be allowed to have her own way. After Gordon disappeared the first time, Miriam felt that she and Bruce had done the right thing in taking Harold, and she did her utmost to convince Bruce that it had all been for the best. After all, they were Harold's next-of-kin and the fact that they took him a few weeks prior to his father's disappearance was really neither here nor there.

A year after Harold's marriage, Vincent was born, but before Vincent had turned ten, Harold, haunted by physical disability, constant pain and the horrendous images that insisted on flitting over that border between his past and present lives, committed suicide. He chose a deserted place near the water, not far from the Power Station, and blew his brains out. A note, later found at home on his side of the bed, had only one word: *Sorry*.

Miriam and Bruce stepped into the void and attempted

to give Vincent and his mother the emotional care that they both desperately needed, while they wondered if Harold's suicide was, in some way, punishment for the dreadful thing they had done so many years previously. Although Vincent and his mother may well have needed sensitive, loving support, they were thankfully not destitute, as Harold's army service guaranteed them a reasonable pension.

Two years later, Bruce died, and Miriam moved in with Vincent and his mother. The year that Vincent turned seventeen, Miriam, who was now well over eighty, was diagnosed with terminal cancer and was given only a couple of months to live. Plagued by thoughts of what she had done and no doubt fearful of eternal retribution, she decided to make some kind of compensation by making a full confession of her crime. She was not what one would call a religious woman, even if she had a very real fear of what might be waiting for her after death. She did not turn to a priest or a minister to make her confession but, instead, to her grandson.

Vincent was understandably shocked to hear that he was actually a Parrish and not a Tyler and that the two people he had grown up with, believing all the time that they were his grandparents, were not his grandparents at all. It took several days for the truth to sink in, a truth about which he was ambivalent. That Miriam had taken care of Harold after Anna had been murdered was admirable; that she had then held on to the child and moved to Sydney, in spite of the fact that it was apparent that Gordon was innocent, was something that Vincent found very difficult to understand, more especially when it became clear that Bruce had been totally against the idea.

Vincent's loyalties were split. Part of him felt that he should resume the Parrish surname, but he had always loved the two people he had accepted as his grandparents; his father had lived and died believing that he was a Tyler; his mother was a Tyler. He knew practically nothing about Gordon Parrish.

In the end, Vincent decided that he was actually neither one nor the other but that it made more sense for him to retain the name his father had always concluded was the family name. He was unable to give Miriam absolution, but he told her that he could understand that in some convoluted way she had meant well.

Miriam eventually died, and whether or not she then had to make peace on the other side with the family whose lives she had completely disrupted must always remain an unanswered question.

Life moved on. Vincent finished school and attended university where he studied psychology and philosophy. Like his father and his real grandfather, he was a quiet, reserved type of boy. He became an academic, and although he had several girlfriends over the years he never married.

When he was in his early twenties, shortly after his mother's death, he travelled to the town and made it his business to find out all there was to know about his grandfather. He visited the property where Gordon had once worked for MacPherson. MacPherson was, of course, long since dead, and the property had been passed on to his son and finally on to his granddaughter. The granddaughter and her husband, neither of whom had very much interest in the land, had seen a way of making a handsome amount of money, and they had sold the property to a neighbour who was wanting to increase his holdings. Although the neighbour was closer in age to

MacPherson's granddaughter, he had known Mac-Pherson's son well. His friendly relationship with the younger MacPherson meant that he had often heard talk both about MacPherson senior and even about Gordon. From what he had picked up, he gathered that Gordon Parrish had been a reliable hard worker and that the accusation of murder had been ill-informed. Like so many others, he came to the conclusion that it was a tragedy that Gordon should have first lost his wife and then his son.

'Enough to make anyone go stark, staring mad,' he said to Vincent.

After talking to the neighbour, Vincent had made his way up on to the ridge and, using a hand-drawn map that the neighbour had given him, he finally managed to find the hut. He was amazed that the hut was still standing after so many years. For Vincent, walking into the hut was almost a spiritual experience. It was all he had that connected him with his grandfather, and, like Doug so many years later, he was very aware that he was now in a space that had been inhabited by Gordon Parrish all those years before. He slid his hand over the few pieces of furniture that remained, his eyes closed, and tried to connect with a man he did not know, but who was such an important part of his life.

Since Vincent had been made aware that he was not really a Tyler and not completely a Parrish, he was not sure who he was. He remained caught between both Tyler and Parrish, not belonging anywhere. As the years passed, he thought a lot about the reality of being, and the extent to which a name cemented that feeling, or reality. Was it Tyler or Parrish that made him the person he was, or was it something else? If he had grown up as Smith or O'Connell would he have been the same or would he have been completely different? What was it that was real, and what was it that was layered over the reality as a kind of fictional response to environmental and even emotional factors? He did not know.

Over the ensuing years, he would often travel out to the town simply to spend time in his grandfather's hut. He would sit on the floor, breathing in the remnants of a time past, and he would try to answer all the questions for which there were no answers. When he was in his fifties he wrote a book, but because he was neither Tyler nor Parrish, he used a pseudonym - V.A. Collins.

The book he wrote was *Virtual Reality and Abstract Truth.*

12

When Evans first heard about Shane in the pub that night so many months ago, he had not been particularly concerned: people disappeared all the time, usually because it was the easiest or, sometimes the only, option available to them. There were lots of reasons why people needed to disappear, many of them eventually reappeared; some never did. He had always expected that Shane would reappear. That was until he learnt about the Germans and Betsy and had experienced the disappearance of Sandra almost at first-hand. He knew it was not really first-hand, he was in no way involved, but the fact that Greg was connected with the office and that he had actually been to the pub with him made it feel like it was first-hand. He could not understand why Doug had not said something about the other disappearances when he had had the opportunity. Before Sandra disappeared.

Not that he was blaming Doug in any way; Evans was well aware that it was very easy to make the wrong choice for all the right reasons. In fact, he was genuinely concerned about Doug: he could see that what he had done, or not done, was constantly preying on his mind. It was almost as though the words "*If only...*" were emblazoned across his forehead. Evans did not have much time for regret: his philosophy was to move on from mistakes. He had made lots of mistakes in his life, and sometimes he had been caught up in the mistakes of others, completely against his will. The last of these mistakes had propelled him from Queensland to New South Wales and eventually to the town. He had chosen the town because of its size, not too large and not too small, and because of its location only a few hours' drive from the capital. If life became too quiet and set in a rut, he knew that there were other options not that far away.

Like Doug, Evans felt that the track had to have something to do with the disappearances. He had seen several sinkholes in Queensland, and he had read that they were not that uncommon in western New South Wales. But he knew that the disappearances had nothing to do with holes suddenly opening up in the track. If that were the case then the holes would still be there, even if the people themselves had disappeared.

He considered the possibility of aliens coming down from outer space and beaming up anyone who just happened to be walking along the track, but he knew that the idea was ridiculous. The fact that his mind was moving off on such tangents was an indication that he was becoming desperate.

For Doug's sake, he really wanted to find Sandra.

***

It was a week or so after Gordon Parrish's remains had been identified. Evans had read all about Gordon and the Tylers in the newspaper, thinking to himself that some people's mistakes could, unfortunately, have unforeseen consequences.

He did not feel that there was any connection between Gordon Parrish and the missing people; it was merely a coincidence that the remains turned up where they did in the middle of an ongoing investigation. The focus for the missing people had to be the track and possibly the ridge; Gordon Parrish was simply a worrisome deviation. After all, Gordon Parrish had died more than seventy years ago.

He thought through all he knew about the missing people. From what he had been told that night at the pub, he knew that Shane had parked his ute a short way along the track. He also knew that when Alf returned to town on his own, and people became concerned about Shane and began backtracking, the keys had been discovered still hanging in the ignition. Shane had never intended to disappear: he had intended to return to the town with his dog. As he always did.

When Evans was later brought up to date on the other three missing people, he was told that the two Germans had evidently veered off from the main road and walked in along the track. It seemed a strange thing to do when they were actually hoping to get a lift, but, on the other hand, they may have needed a toilet break, or perhaps they had noticed something further along the track that, for whatever reason, caught their interest. That one of their backpacks was discovered almost level with the ridge indicated that they had either walked that far of their own free will or that a third person had carried the backpack to where it was later found. Evans could not help wondering: where was the second backpack?

It made sense that Betsy Riley may have ventured up along the track in the hope of receiving better mobile coverage; after all, her car had broken down, and she needed help. He knew that Sandra had walked all the way to the ridge with Greg and that she had then disappeared somewhere beyond the hut. It was this bit of information that continued to perplex Evans - Greg was there; why had he not seen anything? Was it really possible for someone to disappear so completely when there was someone else in the vicinity? Someone who knew them and who should have been looking out for them. Did Greg know more than he was letting on? Was he somehow involved?

Most of the time, Evans did not really think that Greg was involved. He had only met Greg on a handful of occasions, and he found him to be both agreeable and genuine. There were, however, times when he wondered: genuine and agreeable people could also do dreadful things; it was just that it was not immediately apparent.

Although Evans knew nothing about the two men who had been out on the ridge the night that Greg had been there taking photos, he did know about Doug's unpleasant experience in the storm. It was more than possible that the man on the track was completely innocent; however, it was not at all impossible that *someone* was involved in all the disappearances in much the same way that *someone* had been involved in Gordon's disappearance all those years ago.

Like Doug, Evans decided to do some investigation on his own; however, unlike Doug, he was not keen on the idea of physically exploring the track. The disappearances were haphazard, and, in a couple of cases, there were several years between them: he really could not imagine setting up camp out on the track for months on end, waiting for something to happen. As far as Evans was concerned, there had to be other ways of getting the information he needed.

One of the last positions Evans had before he left Queensland was for a surveillance company, monitoring video cameras in a large shopping centre in Brisbane. He was adept at what he did, and during his time with the company he had learnt a lot. He was amazed at what was already possible then, but surveillance had progressed exponentially. He now knew that it was possible to have wire-free, wireless cameras that could be placed almost anywhere to send images, via special software, to all internet-friendly devices. The more he thought about it, the more he was certain that such a camera could perhaps give him the information he needed. If there was someone on the track who should not be there, he would know about it almost immediately.

He did some research and found a camera that, from the glowing product description, sounded as though it would be able to do the job perfectly. It was reasonably small and easy to install, and it could be positioned any-where. The battery lasted for five months, but the camera was also equipped with a solar panel that sent charges to the battery, which resulted in more or less continuous operation. The information obtained was all managed on a secure cloud platform for which there was an ongoing monthly subscription. The camera itself cost almost two thousand dollars.

It was the cost that made Evans baulk a little. There was no way that he could afford so much money, and even if he had been able he was dubious as to whether or not he would be able to bypass the police and set up his own surveillance camera. The only option was to get Senior Constable Dave Bennett on side. Perhaps there was extra funding for this kind of thing, more especially when five people had already disappeared and no one had any idea how or why.

Dave Bennett was sceptical. He agreed with Evans that it could perhaps be a good idea, but he felt that there were too many legal and financial hurdles. Also, as he pointed out, there might not be any more disappearances, and even if there were there was nothing to guarantee that the disappearance would take place exactly in view of the camera. It was a bit like throwing darts at a dart board in the dark.

Evans was disappointed; he would have to come up with a new plan.

While he was still thinking about what he might be able to do, Doug contacted him late one evening, almost in a panic. Any ideas concerning plans or surveillance cameras had completely evaporated long before Doug had even finished speaking.

***

Doug had finally decided to put the missing people behind him, and to that end he had joined the local tennis club. It was definitely nothing fancy: two courts, built sometime in the mid-1900s, and a three-sided shed. He had decided that physical activity and new faces were what he needed. He had not played tennis for years, though he still knew the basic moves; it was just a matter of perfecting his strokes and increasing his physical endurance. Push-ups every morning and a long jog after work of an evening. Doug was already noticing a difference even though he had only been on his new regime for a couple of weeks.

The people at the tennis club were friendly, and,

fortunately for Doug, none of them were in any way connected to anyone who had gone missing. There were no topics of conversation to avoid, no deep holes straddled by difficult silences where a wrong step could send him hurtling to the bottom. There was no sense of guilt, no *if only…*

Although most of the people were new faces, there were two or three whom Doug vaguely knew from those years directly after school when he had been more socially active: it helped him feel less of an outsider. But outsider or not for Doug it was simply a relief to be able to lose himself in superficial conversation and activity where expectations remained at an achievable level. The biggest relief was not having to think about Sandra and the very real possibility that he was somehow responsible for what had happened.

The club met every Tuesday evening and played for two or three hours, depending on the number of people who turned up. Doug was pleased with the progress he was making; on his third visit, he was even on the winning side in a game of doubles, though how much was due to his input and how much was due to the proficiency of his partner was difficult to say.

Afterwards there were cups of tea and some home-made cakes provided by the women in the club. People sat around and talked, about the games, local politics, the weather, then things began to wind down, the left-over cakes were packed away and the cups and plates were washed up. Finally the roller door was pulled down and locked and the lights were turned off. People drifted off with assurances that they would be back again the following week. Most of them were driving, but Doug, as he had done on the two previous occasions, was walking.

It was early June, quite cold and very dry. The courts

were at the very south-west edge of the town, and beyond the courts there was not much more than open paddocks and scattered clumps of bush. After leaving the courts, Doug crossed a small dirt road and reached the main road. Following the road back towards the centre of town, Doug knew that he had a good two-kilometre walk ahead of him.

The sky was filled with stars and there was a full moon, so although it was dark, there being no street lights this far from the centre of town, Doug could easily see where he was going. He was enjoying the physicality of walking, the coldness against his face and the feeling of being the only person on the planet. There was no one else around, and all he could hear was the sound of his tennis shoes on the loose stones beneath his feet. Strange black and grey tree shapes bordered the road, and around him were all the night sounds.

He had been walking for about ten minutes, when he rounded a small bend in the road and noted a shape disengage itself from the line of trees on the right-hand side of the road and begin to move towards him. It was not difficult to see that the shape was a person, even though it was not much more than a collection of dark tones.

Doug was not particularly perturbed: it was not unusual to meet people when he was walking at night.

The collection of tones was moving closer, and Doug could already make out the shape of a face and a body with moving arms and legs. Whoever it was, he – Doug had decided that from the gait and the size it had to be a *he* – was wearing a heavy jacket and a scarf covering the lower part of his face. As they were both walking towards each other at approximately the same speed, Doug calculated that it would not be long before they would be level with each other.

The person was now only metres from him.

Doug raised his hand by way of greeting and was about to say something, but at the same moment the man lifted his head and looked directly at Doug.

Everything inside of Doug froze.

It was Shane.

13

Greg could not get past what Thelma had told him. With every cell in his body he wanted it to be Betsy who had phoned, because that would mean that she was still alive. And if Betsy was still alive then perhaps Sandra was alive as well. But the more he thought about it, the more unlikely it seemed. It was more than a year since Betsy had disappeared, and unless she had been able to recharge her phone it would have died months ago. Although he did not want to admit it to himself, it was likely that the phone had simply been found by someone. Someone who had browsed the address list and who, by pure chance, had then phoned Thelma.

Still, there was a very small chance that Betsy was still alive, that she had somehow been able to recharge the phone and that she had also tried to phone her sister.

He was still seeing the counsellor, and he was finally making some progress, but everything with Thelma and Betsy and the telephone calls was starting to push him backwards. He could feel that he was sliding towards a place where he no longer knew what was real and what was not real. All he really wanted to do was to pull a blanket over his head and completely disappear.

He also began wondering if he had perhaps been too hasty, shelving the idea of connections. Both Dave Bennett and the counsellor had told him that it it was extremely detrimental for him to be going down such a path, but Greg knew that some paths were unavoidable, they were the only way from A to B. Was it possible that identifying the *connections* was the only way of finding Sandra and the others?

Greg moved into this almost forbidden area of thought much like a swimmer approaching the ocean. He tested it cautiously, feeling the cold, knowing that the only way to be in charge was to plunge in; he would not gain anything by standing on the edge, reflecting on the discomfort and the danger. He closed his eyes and remembered how he had isolated the word *loss*. He was not ready to discard the word, but he felt that there had to be other connections: things or events or even characteristics that tied the five people together and that gave some indication as to why they had all disappeared.

That was the way he interpreted the word *connections*, but perhaps he had misunderstood it all. Even while he was searching for some explanation on the only level that made any sense to him, he was uncomfortably aware that the whole thing might be ever so much bigger and might encompass much more than he had ever dreamt.

It was difficult to solve a puzzle that quite obviously stretched beyond the limits of one's own intellect.

After much inner debate, he phoned Dave Bennett and mentioned what Thelma had told him. He knew that Thelma had already spoken to Dave about the phone calls, but he needed to know where the detective stood in relation to this newest piece of evidence. He was hoping that Dave would give him some indication as to whether he believed in the plausibility of what Thelma had told him and whether or not he he intended to do anything about it. From Dave's rather terse answer,

Greg understood that he was sceptical and that he most probably had no intention of following it up.

Caught somewhere between the blanket and the pounding surf, Greg made a hasty decision to visit Thelma. Admittedly it would have to be time without pay, but at least he would not be losing his job.

This time, however, he decided to drive, knowing that Thelma lived a good way out from the town and that he would need transport of his own.

***

He had phoned Thelma several days in advance, though his intuition or sixth sense was telling him that he should not be involving himself in something that was very likely nothing more than an elderly woman's over-wrought imagination. While he was mentally listing all the reasons why he *should* be getting involved, his mood kept swinging between elated and dejected, hopeful and depressed. He was praying that everything would fall into place when he finally met up with Thelma.

It was a Wednesday. He had left Sydney around six in the morning, and he reached the town shortly before midday after a leisurely coffee stop along the way. He drove through the town and continued for another forty kilometres before turning off to the right on to a private road.

The road was unsealed and not much wider than the car. On either side, paddocks stretched as far as Greg could see. A couple of kangaroos hopped across the road in front of him. The melancholy sound of crows was the only sound he could hear except for the car as it bumped over the uneven ground.

After six kilometres, by which time Greg was begin-

103

ning to wonder if perhaps he had turned off the main road too early, the road climbed a rise and there in front of him, behind a row of stark, undressed poplars, was the house.

It was a single-storey weatherboard house, completely surrounded by verandas. At the front of the house there had been some attempt to create a square of lawn and a garden of sorts; further to the right was a conglomeration of sheds and heavy machinery.

Greg pulled up outside the low white fence marking a border between the road and the house area. He stepped out of the car and stretched: the drive had been longer than he had anticipated. He lifted the metal latch on the gate and, closing it behind him, walked up to the house. He could hear a couple of dogs barking, but the barking came from somewhere near the sheds, not the house. He was about to knock on the door when it opened.

Thelma said, 'I heard you arrive.' Then, after an almost unnoticeable pause, she added, 'Come on in.'

Greg followed her down a polished dark timber hall to a sitting room where a fire was burning in the open fireplace. As they walked in, a white cat, lying on the chair closest to the fire, raised its head, eyed Greg up and down, stretched a little and then went back to sleep. Greg sat down in a high-backed leather chair next to a low, doily-covered table while Thelma disappeared to collect the tea things.

She soon returned with a tray on which she had a tea-pot, two cups and saucers, milk, sugar, a couple of plates, some scones and two small bowls with jam and cream. Greg stood up in an attempt to help her with the tray, but Thelma assured him that she had everything under control. As he sat down again, and while she was placing the contents of the tray on the small table, Greg asked, more from a sense of politeness – he had already noted the two cups and plates – if her husband would be joining them.

Thelma shook her head and pointed in a vague direction beyond the house, saying that he was busy with something in the western paddock and that he would be gone for most of the day.

When they were both seated with a cup of tea and a scone, Greg decided to launch into the reason he was there.

'The telephone call... from Betsy.'

'Oh, yes,' she said, 'it was really most strange. Quite unexpected. As I told you before, she just hung up on me.'

'But you were sure that it was Betsy?'

Thelma took a sip of her tea and then said, 'Absolutely. She's the only person who ever calls me Thelmie.'

'Thelmie?'

'You know, Thelmie and Betsy – one of those childish things that stuck I suppose.' She looked into the fire, and then, after a few moments, she looked back at Greg. 'But she hung up... why do you think she hung up on me?'

Greg guessed that there could have been a myriad of reasons as to why she may have hung up, but exactly why she had done so he had no idea. Instead of answering Thelma's question, he asked, 'Her phone... did she phone from her mobile?'

Thelma looked surprised. 'Well, I had assumed so, I mean that was the only phone she had with her, but then he asked me the same question, and–'

'He?' It was Greg's turn to look surprised. 'What do you mean, *he*?'

The woman was slightly hesitant. She said, 'The

policeman... what's his name? Bennett. Yes, Bennett. He asked me exactly the same thing.'

So Dave had not been disinterested at all. For Greg it was like a small epiphany: obviously Dave Bennett had been so concerned about the effect the information might have had on Greg that he had been unable to admit that the phone calls might actually be something worth following up. Greg was not sure whether he should be thankful or angry. He was still trying to decide when Thelma spoke again.

'I showed him the phone,' she said, handing it to Greg, 'and he checked the calls. He said that they hadn't come from Betsy's mobile at all.'

Greg took the phone and checked the inbox. Sure enough, there were two calls from an unnamed caller. The number was listed as private.

Thelma guessed what Greg was thinking. 'Betsy's number is not listed as private, so she must have phoned from another phone,' she said, taking back the phone and placing it in her pocket.

Greg nodded. At least they knew that Betsy did not phone from her own phone, but whether the borrowed phone was a mobile or a landline was anyone's guess.

Thelma was talking again. 'He took my phone, you know. He had it for several days. Not sure if he worked out anything from it, but a nice young policeman brought it back to me the day before yesterday.'

Greg now knew that he needed to talk with Dave Bennett.

Back in the town, Greg checked in at the hotel. He had now been there so many times that everyone working at the hotel knew him, if not by name, at least by appearance. He always took the same room, a small room at the back of the hotel, overlooking the park.

He left his luggage in his room and his car in the hotel car park, having decided to walk to the police station. The afternoon was wearing on, but Greg had a feeling that Dave would still be at work.

Feelings, however, are not always correct, and when he reached the police station, he was told that Detective Senior Constable Dave Bennett was not available but that he should be back within the hour.

Although it was getting close to knock-off time, Greg wandered up to the office on the off-chance of meeting up with Doug before he left for the day. As he entered, Doug and Evans were on their way out, so Greg joined them and the threesome made their way to the local pub.

Greg could not help noticing that Doug was unusually quiet and not really himself. He refrained from saying anything, but when they reached the pub and, ignoring the public bar, found a table in a secluded corner, Greg turned to his colleague and asked, 'Everything okay?'

Doug looked across at Evans and then at Greg. He shook his head and then said, 'I'm not sure... I know it sounds ridiculous, but I saw Shane last night. He was a close as I am to you, so I couldn't possibly have been mistaken. It *was* Shane. He was walking along the road out of town, he– '

Greg interrupted, 'Shane?'

Evans had already gone across to the bar to get some drinks, and Doug continued, 'As I was telling Evans this morning, Shane was walking along the road as though nothing had happened. It was weird, really weird.'

'Did you speak with him? Did he say anything?' Greg could feel the adrenalin surging through his body – first Betsy and now Shane. 'Did he say where he had been? Did he mention the others? Did he mention Sandra?'

Doug shook his head and said, 'No, it was not like that. We didn't talk, not really. I was in a state of shock.' He looked directly at Greg and said, 'I think that he may have said something about it being a lovely evening, and then he simply kept walking.'

Greg was dumbfounded. To be so close and to just let him go. He ventured, a tinge of irritation in his voice, 'But surely you asked him something?'

Doug shook his head. 'You should have been there, Greg; it was not as simple as you might think. It was not a time for asking questions.'

Evans had returned with three schooners of beer. As he sat down, he asked, 'It *was* him, wasn't it? I mean, we all assumed that he was most probably dead.'

Greg immediately picked up on what Evans was hinting at. He looked at him and asked, 'You're wondering whether it was actually Shane or whether it was–'

'His ghost,' finished Evans, taking a mouthful of his beer. He shrugged, 'It probably sounds freaky, but it *is* a possibility.'

It was one of several possibilities. Greg knew that Doug had been worrying overly much about the disappearances, especially since Sandra had gone missing. He had told him numerous times that he was not to blame and that he should not hold himself at all accountable, but words do not weigh much when one has already judged oneself guilty and deserving of punishment. Greg could not help wondering if perhaps Doug had seen someone in the dark and simply assumed that it was Shane. Because he wanted it to be Shane? Because he did not want it to be Shane?

Doug said, 'It was definitely no ghost. He was next to me; I could feel him, not so much physically, but... ' He obviously felt that he was tying himself up into knots. He added, 'I could see his breath; I could smell him; I could hear his boots... '

All three men were silent for a moment, then Doug spoke again, 'There was one thing that I definitely remember: he was wearing a scarf, and even though it was dark I'm sure it was gold, red and black. Of course, I could have been wrong, but it made me think of the two Germans. I couldn't stop wondering if the scarf had actually belonged to one of them.'

14

Greg's mind was trying to process far too many things all at once. Apart from his unexpected meeting with Vincent Tyler, there was Thelma's telephone call from Betsy, and Doug's supposed meeting with Shane. Greg was still unsure as to whether or not Doug had actually seen Shane, after all it had been dark, but his friend had been adamant. If it were true, then it meant that Shane was still alive, and if the telephone call was genuine then perhaps Betsy was alive as well. It followed that if two of the five missing people were still alive then the other three might also be alive.

But none of it made very much sense. Why would Betsy phone her sister and then hang up? Why had Shane been walking along a deserted road in the dark instead of reconnecting with all his friends? Where had Shane and Betsy been all this time? Where were they now?

And what part, if any, was Vincent playing in all of this? Was it simply a coincidence that Greg had seen him in Sydney and then again at the hotel? Greg could accept the fact that Tyler was related to Gordon Parrish and that he was in the town because he was helping the police with identification, but why had Greg stumbled over him all those months ago, and what was the importance of the word *connections*?

Was there some connection between Vincent and the missing people, and, if so, what was it?

Greg began to get a headache from trying to find answers to all these questions. He decided that he needed to empty his head and fill it with something else instead. He needed to push his mind in other directions, and perhaps when he was not thinking about the multitude of questions he could not answer then the answers would simply come to him of themselves.

He had read about half of his book *Virtual Reality and Abstract Truth*. He had been enjoying it, but there had been so many other things fighting for his time that, even on those occasions when he did find a free time slot where he could sit down and read a few pages, his mind had often been elsewhere, focused on all the other things.

He made himself some strong coffee, which he took into the lounge room. Rain was battering at the dark windows, and he was very thankful that he was inside and not outside on such an unpleasant evening. The warm red and orange flames dancing in the combustion heater, his hot drink and the comfortable armchair only underlined his feeling of gratitude. He settled himself in the chair, removed the bookmark from his book and continued to read.

***

It was very late when he finally read the last page and closed the book. He had to admit that it had been extremely interesting, and he was already planning to go back and reread some of the chapters. While he had been reading he had marked a number of the pages with slips of paper on which he had written things like: *I couldn't agree more. Compare with page 134, paragraph 6. What is reality?...*

He had also jotted down a few quotes on a separate piece of paper, and now, having finished the book, he glanced through them, reliving an array of opinions and ideas, many of which were not new and some of which were in complete contradiction to his own way of thinking. All the suggestions needed time to be absorbed. Eventually they would be weighed against other views and interpretations, both his own and those he had assimilated from others, and there was a good chance that they would be reassessed and even altered. But, for the moment at least, many of them still felt new, exciting and thoroughly plausible.

Greg's thoughts played around with the concepts of absolute and virtual, of abstract and real. He felt that on some level he could relate to Collins' idea of abstract truth. It made sense that if truth were absolute then everything, indeed life itself, would in all probability be quite terrifying. Absolute truth would mean that there could be no room to deviate sideways, backwards or even forwards: there would be no *perhaps*, no grey areas: everything would have to be either absolutely black or absolutely white. But, on the other hand, if there was no absolute, no central structure to which everything else could cling, then the result would most probably be chaos.

He wondered if truth could perhaps be absolute in essence while still having an abstract or hypothetical veneer. After considering the concept for a few minutes – he liked the idea of an abstract veneer – he decided that he was probably trying to manipulate reality to fit his own agenda. Nevertheless, although it was a fairly clear-cut truth that it was light during the day and dark at night, it was impossible to ignore the fact that, depending on where one lived on the globe, this truth was not necessarily always absolute: there were other factors that could completely negate the obvious.

It was similar with colours. Most people would agree that the colour green was an absolute, but it could only ever be superficially absolute. It could never be completely absolute as long as there were people who looked at that particular colour and saw a colour that most other people called red or blue or yellow. Everyone could point at the colour green and say green, but there was a disparity between the different perceptions of what green actually was. The strange thing, Greg thought, was that no one would probably ever know that the perceptions were different, because everyone believed that what he or she was looking at was green. In all cases green could be called a kind of absolute truth, but after being processed by different brains, the perception itself was very different.

This flexibility of perception fascinated Greg, and he had to admit to himself that it had not been something to which he had previously given much thought. Of course he was aware that people had different likes and dislikes, but the idea of two people looking at the same thing and calling it by the same name while perceiving it completely differently enthralled and excited him. How could he, or anyone, know what the person next to him was actually seeing or perceiving. When Greg observed his neighbour sitting on his front veranda, looking out at the street, there was nothing saying that his neighbour was looking at the street in the same way as he, Greg, might be looking at the street. Perhaps his neighbour's perception had nothing at all to do with the shapes and forms in front of him and more to do with emotions or colours or something else entirely. Or perhaps, while Greg might say that he saw a man and a woman walking along the street, his neighbour might be completely focused on a bird sitting in a bush on the other side of the road. Greg's experience might centre around two people on a street, but the neighbour's experience need not have anything at all to do with people. In fact, it could be more than likely that he may not even have seen them. For the neighbour, the people did not exist; they were not part of his reality. For Greg, the bird did not exist.

Greg thought back to something he had read in the book: *certain truths might be considered absolute, but the perception of truth is another thing altogether.*

He leant back in the armchair, trying to sum up for himself what the book was all about. It was definitely about the perception of truth and whether or not truth as such could be absolute, but it was also about the need for balance between illusion and reality and what happens when this balance is affected.

What we see is not necessarily reality and what is considered reality might not be what we are actually seeing.

As far as Greg was concerned, the two things, truth and reality, were definitely related. The truth of any reality confronting each and every one of us was always filtered through individual perceptions of that particular reality. In actual fact there were possibly as many realities and truths as there were people. Perhaps what he was experiencing, at this very moment, as being real might appear as a very different reality when perceived through someone else's eyes and intellect.

He stood up, turned off the heater and the lights, and made his way to the bedroom. There were only a few hours of night left, and he would very soon have to get up to go to work.

On his way to the bedroom, he wondered: is reality palpable or can it never be anything more than an illusion filtered through a multitude of different perceptions? Is what is happening *actually* real, or is it always connected to our imagination and the sum of our intellectual and emotional experiences? Am I here in this house, on my way to bed, or am I actually somewhere else, doing something completely different?

***

The next morning, the rain had stopped, and the sun was making a feeble, but cold, reappearance. Greg managed to be up and dressed no later than usual, and by seven-thirty he had already left the house. After a short walk to the station, he took the train into the city. Although he normally did not commence work until nine, he had a couple of loose ends he needed to get out of the way before the day started in earnest.

By the time he had worked his way through his must-be-done-before-I-start-work pile, the rest of the office staff had arrived, and Greg found himself swept up in the general daily bustle of the office. There were claims to draw up, claims to process and clients to see. In between these different activities, there were the many cups of coffee and the very occasional few moments of inactivity when he stood at his window on the twenty-first floor, looking out over the city below.

At twelve-thirty Greg decided that he had earned a break, and taking his coat he left the office, rode the lift down to the ground floor and stepped out on to the footpath.

His right shoe felt looser than normal, and he stopped near the façade of the next-door building and tied his lace. The shoes and the laces were new, but the laces did not grip particularly well; perhaps he would have to do something about getting other, more dependable, laces.

The sun had actually picked up in strength during the morning, and the day was quite pleasant with a cloudless blue sky and a temperature that felt more like early spring than midwinter. Greg decided to take a train to Circular Quay and grab a sandwich for his lunch. If he had luck, he might find a free bench outside the Museum of Contemporary Art where he could enjoy the unusually beautiful weather and watch the boats on the water.

He entered the underground train station and stepped on to the escalator going down to his platform. It was a very long, steep escalator, but it was also fairly old, and the treads covering the metal steps were timber and widely spaced.

As he stepped on to the escalator, his mind was filled with a conglomeration of thoughts about work, Sandra, reality, truth, Vincent Tyler... and, for whatever reason, he tripped.

And he fell.

Whether he had simply overbalanced, whether he had placed his foot wrongly on the stair or whether his lace had loosened again and had then either become caught in the mechanism or trapped under his other foot, he never knew. He was not holding on to the handrail. There was absolutely nothing to stop his fall.

The escalator was a very long downward plunge of moving stairs, and there was only one other person in front of him, a long way down.

It was like falling from the top of a high cliff.

He could feel the sharp edges of the steel steps as they knocked against his legs, his arms, his body, his head. He did not have time to fully appreciate what was actually happening.

Then, suddenly, he could feel nothing at all.

The people who had run to the foot of the escalator moved back as the platform guard shoved his way to the front, mobile in hand, asking for immediate assistance, pushing the emergency switch on the escalator.

A man came forward and said he was a nurse. A woman was already kneeling next to Greg, trying to find a pulse.

A man, holding on to a maroon suitcase, stood a little to one side of the group of incredulous, curious, shocked people.

The woman on the ground was shaking her head. It did not seem as though there was very much that could be done.

The man lying on the cold, grey platform at the bottom of the escalator was almost certainly dead.

15

Greg leant over and touched his wife gently on her arm. It was already seven in the morning, and as much as he would like to have remained in bed he knew that he had a train to catch. He sat up and swung his feet down to the floor.

'I'll try to finish a little earlier this evening,' he said, 'perhaps we could have dinner somewhere in the city?'

Sandra was still half asleep. She murmured something that he missed and then pulled the quilt more tightly around her.

Greg showered and dressed. While his coffee was brewing, he repeated what he had suggested earlier about eating out that evening. Sandra was still lying in bed, but now she was more or less awake, and she agreed with Greg that it could be a nice change. She was doing an afternoon shift, but she said that she should be able to meet him at his office around five-thirty.

Later, sitting on the train on his way to work, Greg looked out the window at the houses rushing past. His mind was in neutral: he was aware of everything around him, but he was dissociated, separate. It was a state that he seldom enjoyed. Too often there were work problems to solve and a multitude of other things to wade through: things like a leaking tap in the laundry that needed fixing, his state of health, a problem at work, what to do on the weekend, the political situation, the worrying sound that had suddenly invaded the car engine, whether he was spending too little time with his wife...

He enjoyed being in neutral, and although he was not aware of it (otherwise he would have been worrying) he enjoyed being temporarily free of problem-solving. But his mind was not completely empty; his thoughts were moving slowly and rhythmically in and around the events of the past six months. It was all very similar to a handful of leaves floating on sparkling, sunlit water. There was no sense of obligation; everything was extremely peaceful.

He thought back to January when he and Sandra had taken a few days off from work and travelled to Canberra. It had been a very successful holiday, and they had both enjoyed spending time in the capital, doing all the things that tourists do and a whole lot of other things as well. There had been a wonderful exhibition at the National Gallery - some European painter whose name he could no longer remember - while the visit to the War Memorial had simply affirmed what he had always claimed: war definitely needed to be abolished. But then again there had always been war, and it was unlikely that humankind, with some kind of warmongering gene that refused to evolve into something compassionate, would ever change. Saddened by the pictorial reality of the conflicts spread out before him, he decided that the reason why the gene was unable to mutate into something kinder was because it was somehow inexorably bound to an unexplainable hankering after power and control.

The leaves were swaying slowly, probably from a small ripple caused by a bird skimming the water just out of sight.

Thinking about power made him remember Parliament House and how he and Sandra had been part of a tour group, walking behind a guide who seemed to know absolutely everything about the place: when it was built, why and how. He also seemed to know a lot about the different prime ministers and politicians. While listening to the guide, they had walked in and out of beautifully presented rooms, admiring the timber, the marble and the extensive art collection.

Greg's mind was moving in a circle: it had already left Parliament House far behind and was back at the word *compassion*.

The train had stopped at a station, and Greg was vaguely aware of people getting off and other people getting on, but his thoughts continued, defying the ripple.

After Canberra, they had driven east and followed the coast road back to Sydney. It had been a relaxing break, but since then it had been work, work and more work. He moved slightly in his seat, closer to the window, as a woman in a severe business suit sat down beside him.

Nonetheless, he felt that all the work had been worth his while. He had been promoted in March, and there had been a not-to-be-laughed-at salary increase, but he was beginning to feel that it was probably time for another break or holiday. Brisbane or even further north could be the place to be now that winter had well and truly wrapped itself around Sydney. He would see if he could get time off in July, and he would talk about it with Sandra over dinner.

He also needed to tell her that he would be away for a couple of days at the end of the week, his biannual trip to the town.

***

Sandra was already sitting in the reception at Trust Us Insurance when Greg came out of his office at twenty to six. The beauty parlour where she worked part time was halfway between where they lived and the city, and she had phoned Greg when she was on her way into the city.

They left the office, and, after taking the lift to the ground floor, they decided to eat at a small Turkish restaurant in Darling Harbour. They had eaten there once before and had enjoyed both the food and the atmosphere.

The evening was cold, and the lights from hundreds of skyscraper windows and neon signs glittered as they made their way away from the central business district towards the water. It was when they were crossing Pyrmont Bridge that Sandra took Greg by the arm and said:

'That man there, the one with the suitcase, I'm sure that I've seen him before.'

Greg followed the direction of her gaze and saw a tall, middle-aged, grey-haired man pulling a maroon suitcase on wheels. A strange, tingling sensation coursed through his body, down his spine and out to the very tips of his fingers. There was something about the man, but he could not work out what it was. He was positive he had not seen him before, or had he?

He asked, needing to say something, 'Here in the city?'

Sandra nodded. 'A couple of times actually. And both times he had that suitcase with him.'

Greg was still trying to remember if and where he had seen the man. He said, 'There *is* something- '

But Sandra, suddenly entranced by the lights dancing

across the water, had run to the opposite side of the bridge.

'Aren't they absolutely wonderful!' she exclaimed, the man with the suitcase already forgotten.

Greg smiled at her as he took her hand. Yes, they were wonderful, he thought, but fifty percent of his brain was still concentrated on the man with the suitcase. The more he thought about it, the more he became certain he *had* seen him before; perhaps he had even spoken with him...

For some reason, the names *Victor* and *Taylor* pushed their way into his head, but they did not mean anything to him, and, having reached the end of the bridge, he let Sandra go ahead and then followed her down the stairs.

***

Two days later, Greg was back in the town. When he was there last it had been midsummer, the grass had been yellow and brown, and the sun had been burning in a clear blue sky. Now the grass was green after heavy falls of winter rain, and white clouds were blowing across the sky. Also, it was very cold.

He checked in at the hotel where he normally stayed when he was in the town, wrapped himself in his overcoat and scarf and walked across to the office.

Doug, the most senior person in the office, took him into the meeting room where the receptionist had just organized coffee and home-made cake. He closed the door behind them and looked at Greg, a frown creasing his forehead. 'I must say, Greg,' he said, 'I'm quite confused. I can honestly say I wasn't expecting you this time. Last we heard, you were in hospital after some really awful accident. I mean, they weren't even sure if you... why, it's only a couple of days since we sent you flowers.' He paused for a moment before continuing, 'But you seem quite okay, perhaps- '

Greg had removed his overcoat and scarf and had taken a chair at the over-large table. 'Flowers? Accident? What kind of accident? What on earth are you talking about?'

Doug pulled out a chair and sat down opposite Greg. He was feeling as though they were participating in two different films. He said, 'I think it had something to do with an escalator... '

It was difficult to work out what Greg was thinking, but Doug could see that he did not believe the story about escalators and hospitals. Nothing was making any sense. He knew that Jocelyn had arranged for flowers to be sent to the hospital and that they had all signed the card. Head office had phoned and given them the news. At that stage it was dubious as to whether or not Gregory Payne would pull through. Even if he did survive, the consensus of opinion was that it would be months before he would be back in the office, and yet here he was, sitting across the table from him without a mark to be seen.

After a short silence, Greg said, 'I'm not sure what's going on here, but there's been no accident, I've not been in hospital and from what I can gather we've a lot of work to get through.' He reached across the table and pulled the pile of files closer to where he was sitting.

Doug tried to push the wall of questions to the back of his mind and, instead, concentrate on the work in front of them. In spite of Greg's strangely blasé attitude, it was becoming obvious to Doug that he was at least a little distracted, even irritated, and that he was making a concerted, somewhat artificial, effort to appear normal.

'Anything much been happening here?' Greg asked as Doug poured coffee for them both.

Doug replaced the coffee pot on the table and pointed at the files that were now sitting in front of Greg. 'Not a lot,' he said.

Greg took a piece of the cake and, looking at the files, said, 'I was actually thinking of *here*, in the town. I remember, when I was here last, you mentioned something about someone who had gone missing; did he ever turn up?'

Doug had been about to take a mouthful of coffee, but he left the mug standing on the table. 'No,' he said slowly, 'nor did the other four.' He paused for a moment and then continued, 'I don't suppose... I guess you haven't heard from Sandra?'

Now it was Greg's turn to look amazed. 'Well, I spoke to her this morning... '

Doug was not sure why, but he felt as though whatever film he was part of had a lot to do with quicksand. He looked directly at Greg and said, 'But she's missing... or did she turn up?' He was now extremely confused. He said, 'We didn't know, I'm so- '

Greg frowned. 'Missing? What on earth are you talking about? First you have me in hospital and now you're saying that Sandra has gone missing?'

Even if it was only a make-believe film, Doug could still feel the quicksand pulling at his feet, and he was terrified that he was going to disappear beneath the surface at any moment. On second thoughts, he felt that disappearing might be the better of two alternatives; staying in the room with Greg was becoming more and more uncomfortable with every passing minute.

'Yes, missing,' he said. 'This is getting really weird, Greg; she's been missing since January when you both walked out to the ridge.'

Greg was obviously annoyed. 'The ridge? January?' He pushed back his chair and, looking directly at Doug, said, 'I've absolutely no idea what you're talking about, Doug. If all of this is some kind of joke, it is in very poor taste.' He paused for a moment and then, in a quieter voice, continued, 'The only explanation is that there's been some kind of mistake – a mix-up.'

'There's definitely been no mix-up. Why, you've been out here several times since January, and we've been searching all over the place. Just ask Dave Bennett.'

'Dave who?' Although Greg could have no way of knowing anything about Doug's sensation of sinking in soft, sucking, cinematic quicksand, he may well have felt that he was being pulled towards a similar fate.

'Dave Bennett, the detective working on the case,' said Doug.

Greg ran his hands through his hair and said, 'I have absolutely no idea what's going on, but I can assure you that Sandra is definitely not missing. She has not been missing, not now and not at any time in the past. The last time I was here was in January. I did not explore the ridge with Sandra. I have never been anywhere near the ridge, and I can assure you that I do not know anyone called Dave Bennett.'

Doug felt that his head had already disappeared beneath all the mud. 'Something's just not adding up. I can only say what I know, Greg. You and Sandra went out to the ridge in January, and Sandra disappeared; since then the police and God-knows-who have been out looking for her.' He stopped speaking for a moment, breathed in deeply and then continued, 'Though, of course, I may have misunderstood something. I mean, it's always possible... '

Doug's confusion and discomfort were unmistakable, and possibly Greg understood this, because he shrugged and said, 'This is all completely beyond me. Perhaps we should call in and see this Bennett fellow later today?'

Doug's face showed a flicker of relief; he would finally have someone to back up his story. He nodded at Greg and attempted to smile as he pushed the coffee things to one side of the table and opened up the first folder on the pile. 'We should be able to see him after lunch,' he said, 'but first we should probably make some headway on these files.'

***

Detective Senior Constable Dave Bennett came out into the reception area of the police station, acknowledging Doug with a nod of his head. He had not heard of Greg's accident, and he approached Greg with his hand held out, 'Hello, Greg,' he said. 'Was it something in particular? By the way, we may finally have something on that phone Betsy used. I'm hoping it might lead to something positive. The first real break- '

Greg was dumbfounded: the detective obviously knew him or thought he knew him. Greg's thoughts swung back to earlier in the day when Doug was talking about things that made absolutely no sense, and where the words *detective* and *case* were somehow connected with *Sandra* and *missing* and were managing to conjure up a whole lot of images that he really felt that he could do without.

Greg looked at Dave Bennett and then at Doug before finally moving his gaze back to the detective. He was completely and utterly confused.

He interrupted, 'I'm really awfully sorry, but I have

absolutely no idea who you are. In fact, I have never seen you before in my life.'

16

Dave was speechless. The words "I have never seen you before in my life" kept ringing in his ears as he stood, looking from Greg to Doug and then back to Greg.

When he recovered his voice, he said, 'I really don't understand, Mr Payne; we've been searching for your wife all year; you've actually been here–'

Greg interrupted, 'Many times. That's what Doug says as well, but I swear I have not been here since January, and my wife, Sandra, she's definitely not missing. I can swear to that as well.'

'The track, the ridge, the search parties, Thelma, even Vincent Tyler... ' This was a completely new experience for Dave, and he was not at all sure how he should act. Obviously Greg had gone over the edge, but there had to be something with which he could still connect, something that would pull him back to reality. The question was finding it.

Greg closed his eyes and sighed very deeply. When he opened them again, he spoke firmly, with more than a tinge of the anxiety he was doubtlessly feeling. 'No, none of it means anything to me, because I wasn't here. I didn't experience it. I'm sorry if this throws some kind of virtual spanner into the works, but there is not much I can do about it.'

Dave could now see that the last six months had been

too much for Greg, and he wondered how he would have reacted had it been *his* wife who had disappeared all those months ago. It must have been an unbelievably stressful time for Greg, not knowing if his wife was dead or alive, not knowing if he would ever see her again. This had been going on for months now, and there was still nothing that even resembled a light at the end of the tunnel. It was not particularly strange that Greg had finally keeled over. Completely.

Dave wondered what Doug was thinking, but with Greg standing in front of them both, neither could give any indication of their actual thoughts. Dave decided to back down; there would be time for explanations later.

The detective said, 'Doubtlessly there's been some weird mistake – mistaken identity and all that kind of thing.' He was smart enough to realize that there was no point pushing something that, for whatever reason, was completely beyond Greg's comprehension. He paused for a moment and then said with the slightest hint of a smile, 'There must be more than one person called Greg.'

'Of course, it has to be a mistake, and a pretty serious one if you don't mind my saying. I'm Gregory Payne, though most people call me Greg,' said Greg, relieved that someone was actually taking him at his word, and yet strangely unaware that the detective had already referred to him by his surname. 'I work for Trust Us Insurance. Sydney office.'

Dave nodded. 'So you're here to check up on the boys in the office?' he laughed, openly trying to catch Doug's eye.

Before Greg had a chance to say anything, Doug's voice broke into the conversation. 'That's about it it, Dave,' he said, looking directly at Dave and acknowledging all the questions the detective was unable to put into words. 'We'd best be getting back to the office,' he said, 'but I'll drop by again in a few days' time.'

Something resembling a small wave of relief washed over Dave's face: at least they would then be able to talk about what might have happened to Greg and why he was suddenly acting so strangely.

***

Dave Bennett was quite certain that Greg fully believed that Sandra was no longer missing, though what it was that had instigated such a belief, Dave had absolutely no idea. It seemed as though Greg may actually have had contact with her or with someone who looked like her, or perhaps, which was ever so more likely, he had reached the limits of his endurance, and he had fallen, head first, into some kind of fantasy where everything was exactly the way he wanted it to be: no one was missing; in fact, no one had ever been missing. Dave remembered telling Greg months ago that he needed help, and he believed that Doug had mentioned something about Greg seeing a counsellor. Assuming that Doug was correct, then Greg probably needed to change his counsellor, or perhaps he needed to take a step up the mental-health ladder and see a psychiatrist.

There was no other explanation for Greg's behaviour, which, as far as Dave was concerned, had to be tied up with his very fragile mental state.

In the meantime, Dave decided that he would continue as though nothing had happened. As far as the case was concerned, the meeting between himself and Greg had never taken place. The detective knew that he would have to keep a very low profile; it would never do for

Gregory Payne to realize that the police had ignored him and were still searching for his wife.

Dave was a traditionalist when it came to policing. He had more than thirty years of experience behind him, and during that time he had managed to establish routines based on discipline and meticulous procedure. He followed trails of evidence with such determined accuracy and precision that those around him secretly labelled him as having an obsessive-compulsive disorder. Once he had a case to solve, he usually did not falter until he had procured a result and had then tied up all the ends; however, this persistence and singularity of focus was often a cause of irritation between himself and his colleagues. He was well aware that his approach could be exasperating to others, but he knew that it usually achieved results. If, in spite of his determination, he failed to solve a case he would nearly always experience the failure as a personal defeat, spending hours analysing where and why he may have gone wrong.

He really hoped that this would not be the case with Sandra and the four other missing people.

David Gerard Bennett had grown up in Sydney with a father who was a police officer and a mother who was a nurse. His sister followed his mother into nursing and Dave joined the police force. The siblings' career choices were as obvious as the sun rising in the morning and setting in the evening; there had never been any discussion about possible alternatives, and Dave did not contemplate doing anything else. Fortunately, it was an excellent choice as far as Dave was concerned: he related straight away to the discipline, the routine and the structure. After the initial training, he was posted to an inner-city police station where he remained for several years before being moved to a station in one of

Sydney's western suburbs. By the time he had served six or seven years as a uniformed officer, he had already decided that he wanted to move sideways into the detective branch. The process was long, but for Dave not frustratingly so, and after three more years, including a year of specialist training, he finally reached his goal.

He spent a few years back in the inner city and was then moved to a semi-rural area south of the city, by which time he was married with three half-grown children. He was surprised at how well he fitted into the laid-back atmosphere of a small community, and when the chance came for a move to the town he applied and was accepted. The station was relatively small, and while he was the senior constable he was the only detective. Referred to as Senior Constable, Detective Senior Constable and even, occasionally, Constable, Dave placed little importance on titles; as far as he was concerned, the most important thing was the job and not what he was called.

Dave thought back to the meeting earlier in the day. There was no explanation for Greg's behaviour, but no matter what Greg was insisting, Dave knew that he would never give up on Sandra or the others. They had managed to trace Betsy's call to a public phone box in a small community about fifty kilometres north-west of the town. Even though the trail stopped there, they were confident that they had finally pushed their toe inside the door, and things would hopefully begin to open up. He needed to talk to Doug again about the sighting of Shane; they had searched the entire town without coming up with anything. Dave wanted to believe that Doug had seen him, but it had been night and perhaps Doug, like Greg, was slipping into some kind of fantasy world.

***

Doug turned up at the station a couple of days later, more than a little interested to hear what Dave thought about Greg's performance, and whether or not he might have an explanation for what was going on. Dave was just as baffled as Doug, and the two of them spent some minutes turning the meeting with Greg inside out and upside down. No matter how they looked at it, there did not seem to be any logical explanation for what had happened.

The only possible explanation was that Greg had finally had enough.

Dave listed all the conversations he had had with Greg, both face to face and on the phone. He remarked several times that it made absolutely no sense that Greg could stand in front of him and say that he had never seen him before. However, when Doug mentioned Greg's accident and the phone call from head office, Dave became extremely concerned. Things seemed to be spiralling completely out of everyone's control. If Greg was lying in hospital critically injured, he could hardly be visiting them in the town.

Doug agreed, thinking back over Greg's two-day visit. They had worked their way through most of the things that had to be done, but at no point did Greg give any sign that the accident had actually happened, nor did he indicate that he had changed his mind about Sandra.

Later, on the way to the airport, Doug had said, 'You know where I am if you need to talk.'

Greg had laughed and said, 'That's really kind of you, Doug, but there's nothing that I can think of, to talk about that is.' At the airport, he had stepped out of the car before collecting his things from the boot. Shouldering his bag, he had then walked back to Doug's window. 'I really do appreciate your concern, Doug, but Sandra is not missing and never has been.'

Doug had watched him as he disappeared into the very small terminal building. How did one convince someone that his wife was missing when, according to that person, she was not missing?

Dave was talking again, wondering if there was anything at all they could do to help Greg.

Doug said, 'There is one thing I could do: I could visit him in Sydney. If Sandra's there, then at least we'll know that he is telling the truth; if she's not, then we should probably think about getting help for him. There may have been some mistake about the accident; perhaps it was someone else. I probably need to get on to head office and find out what's going on. At this moment in time, I feel that it is one small step at a time. First we have to ascertain whether or not Sandra is in Sydney.'

Dave nodded. A phone rang, and the two men shook hands before Doug left the station.

***

As he had already been there once before, Doug had no trouble finding Greg's house. He had taken a train to the closest station and then walked a kilometre to the free-standing brick house surrounded by a rather lovely garden.

There was an air of solitude resting over the house, but the more Doug looked at the place, the more he felt that the word solitude was not sufficient, abandonment was closer to the mark. There were several local papers lying on the front lawn, and Doug noticed some gaudy advertising material sticking out of the letterbox.

He unlatched the gate and walked up the path to the front door.

He rang the doorbell. There were no sounds coming from inside the house, only the chiming of the doorbell. The short electronic melody came to an abrupt end, and Doug rang again. There was still no answer, and Doug was pretty sure that there was no one at home.

A man from the house next door was on his way to his garage, jiggling his car keys in his hand.

Doug walked back down the front steps and crossed over the grass to the low timber fence. He called out, 'Excuse me, I'm looking for Gregory Payne.'

The man with the car keys, came over to the fence, shaking his head. 'You're a friend of his?'

Doug nodded and explained that they were far-flung work colleagues.

The car-key jiggler suddenly looked quite serious. 'It was all quite dreadful, especially after what happened to his wife.'

Doug could feel a cold sensation in the back of his neck. 'Dreadful?'

'The fall. At first, they thought he was dead, but when the ambulance fellows arrived they actually found a pulse and rushed him to the hospital. He's still there. His sister stopped by a few days ago; she said he'll be okay, but he's been badly hurt. Broken bones everywhere... '

Doug's mouth felt dry. In a voice that he hardly recognized, he asked the neighbour, 'When did this happen?'

The neighbour thought for a few moments, and then he said, 'Two, three weeks ago. It's probably closer to three now, you know how it is with time.'

Doug was unable to answer; it was as though his speaking mechanism had simply laid off completely. He thought how it was barely a week since he last saw Greg, and he was not injured and, according to Greg, Sandra was not missing and never had been missing.

17

Vincent felt that with the discovery of his grandfather's remains a part of his life was slowly beginning to unravel. He was still Tyler, but now everyone knew he was also Parrish. To a certain extent, he had enjoyed being neither one nor the other: it had given him a feeling of being exclusive, different. Although he had no intention of changing his surname, he regretted that he was no longer in charge of his secret. It had ceased to be just his: everyone now knew that he was the son of the boy who had been so cruelly abducted. Vincent thought of Miriam and conceded to himself that although the action had been cruel as far as Gordon was concerned, Harold had never really suffered as a result of what Miriam had done.

Or had he?

Vincent wondered how his father might have turned out had he been reunited with Gordon. Gordon's life would certainly have been very different, Vincent was sure of that, but he, Vincent, would never have seen the light of day. If Vincent agreed that Miriam's action had been unforgivable, he was more or less negating himself. He decided that things happen for a reason, and although he felt extremely sorry for Gordon he really did not want to think himself into oblivion.

He was concerned about Greg, but he felt that there

was not much else he could do for him. He had given him the key, and it was up to Greg to make use of it.

But he was becoming less and less sure that Greg knew how to make use of it.

He should have spoken with him at the hotel even though time had been so tightly compressed. From the little Vincent had seen of Greg, he believed that he was like a boat without oars, moving rapidly into dangerous waters. He had only seen the man three times - or was it four? - but it was more than sufficient for Vincent to have been able to make up his mind about Greg.

The last time he had seen him had been on Pyrmont Bridge, and he was almost certain that Greg had not recognized him. It was there on the bridge that Vincent had begun to suspect that things were not going well for Greg, because, by all rights, Greg should not have been there.

Vincent knew that he needed to do something, but he was still not completely sure as to what he should do. He was very aware that he himself was being pulled between two realities and that one of them was definitely not his. It was a situation he had often thought about, but not one that he had actually experienced. Usually the perception and interpretation of reality was individual, although there were special cases where several people, for whatever reason, were able to share the same perception and interpretation. Vincent was not sure why he had been dragged into Greg's perception as some kind of bystander, fully aware but not active. It was extremely important that Greg could be pulled back into the real world, a world where his wife had disappeared and where he was now fighting for his life. If this were not possible, or if it did not happen very soon, then it was more than likely that Greg would go completely mad. As people began to question his interpretation of everything around him, which they would definitely do, he would no longer know for sure what was real and what was in his mind or in his imagination. Physically and mentally, he would be inhabiting two, or even more, realities, which would eventually have to collide with each other. If nothing were done to rectify the situation, sooner rather than later, it would be difficult to know who was the real Greg and who was the impostor.

He accepted that there could perhaps be some similarities between Greg and himself, caught as he was between two names, but Greg was completely straddled between two realities, which was a very different thing.

Vincent was sitting on a bench in the Botanic Gardens, looking out over the water. Further around to his left was the Sydney Opera House, the white tiles covering its sails gleaming in the bright winter sun. This was one of his favourite spots: a place where he could sit and think without being disturbed.

He decided that he could actually understand Greg. After he had discovered that he was both a Parrish and a Tyler, he lost contact with reality for a while. Was his reality Tyler, or was it Parrish? He had not been completely sure. When he had tried to sum himself up mentally, he decided that he was neither Tyler nor Parrish; he was someone else. All attempts to stand out-side of himself and view himself from someone else's perspective gave exactly the same result: he was no longer sure at whom he was actually looking.

Though there were some vague similarities, Greg's situation was drastically different. It was obvious to Vincent from his very few meetings with Greg, and from what he had read in the newspapers, that Greg *knew* that he was Gregory Payne and that, as Gregory Payne, he had a good job and a lovely wife. Up until January, his life had been mapped out in front of him. It was rather predictable, but that was probably how Greg liked things to be. Vincent guessed that Greg disliked the unexpected and that he most probably found it almost impossible to accept that Sandra was no longer part of the picture. Greg was clinging on to a reality that no longer existed.

The reality of Greg and Sandra.

As long as Sandra was missing, Greg was in a kind of limbo where he could imagine whatever he wanted. He was creating a reality where everything was the way it had always been. Nothing had changed.

Vincent stood up and began to walk towards the Opera House. Realities changed all the time; it was impossible to hold on to just one of them and ignore all the others.

***

Vincent had not spoken with Senior Constable Dave Bennett since his visit to the town for the identification of his grandfather's remains. He had not had any reason to contact him: it had been established beyond any doubt that the remains belonged to Gordon Parrish, and as far as both Dave and Vincent were concerned there was really nothing more to discuss. But Vincent knew that Dave was in charge of the missing persons' case, and he also knew that he was intermittently in contact with Greg. Perhaps he might have some idea of Greg's state of mind and how he was managing.

When he phoned Bennett, he was not at all sure as to what he was going to say; after all, Gregory Payne was not his business. However, he need not have worried; the detective sounded pleased to hear from him and asked him if he was planning another visit.

Vincent assured Dave that he had no such plans for the foreseeable future, but he was interested in hearing how things were going, regarding the five missing people, and if there had been any significant breakthroughs.

Dave was quiet for a moment, and Vincent suspected that he was weighing up what he could tell him and what would have to remain confidential. Then, as if he had carefully thought it all through and come to a decision, he told Vincent that Greg had recently visited the town.

'But the really strange thing was he didn't know me,' continued Dave in a fairly strained voice, 'and what was really, really weird was that he claimed that Sandra was not missing and never had been missing.'

Vincent Tyler felt a chill move through his body, a bit like a ripple moving slowly down from his head to his feet. He thought back to his musings about how Greg was most probably bestriding two different realities. He told Dave that he knew for certain that Greg was still in hospital.

'Just by chance, I happened to be there on the platform when he fell; it was a pretty awful fall. Of course, I'm not in a position to get information from the hospital, but it's been in the papers – you know the kind of thing they write: "Husband of missing woman in near-death experience." From what I have been able to gather, he's still in a pretty bad way.'

The detective sounded stressed, 'But he was here; at least, I think he was here... if it wasn't Payne, then who was it?' He was quiet for a moment before continuing, 'But he looked like Payne, spoke like Payne. He seemed to know Doug... '

Tyler felt as though he had suddenly landed in a very small space where the walls were moving in on him;

very soon he would no longer be able to breathe. There were so many things he could have said, but he knew that none of them would make much sense to a man as practical and mundane as Dave Bennett. Most of them did not really make much sense to him, and he had spent a good deal of his life studying and thinking about ideas and concepts beyond what was normally accepted.

If Greg was lying bandaged in a hospital bed, then there was no way he could be walking around in a town hundreds of kilometres from the hospital. Vincent was fully aware of what was acceptable and feasible, but he also knew that it was possible to experience different realities in tangent to each other. Greg was physically unable to move anywhere at the moment, but his mind was perfectly free to wander wherever it wanted. It made sense to Vincent that Greg had created a reality more in keeping with how he wanted things to be: Sandra was not missing; he had not been injured; life was completely normal. All the stress of the last few months had finally vanished. Vincent could understand all of this, but that such an imagined reality could include other people was something that he had not reckoned with. The other people were all simply bystanders, each of them with their feet planted firmly in their own reality while they were being forced to participate in Greg's imagined reality.

Vincent understood that Dave Bennett was perturbed and stressed, but how could he say to him that Greg was probably split between two realities.

It had been quiet in the phone for some time and Dave must have thought that Vincent had hung up. He broke into Vincent's reverie with a sharp, 'Are you still there?'

Vincent apologized and then said, 'I've really no idea

what's going on. I'm sure that there is an answer somewhere, but- '

Dave interrupted, 'We saw him; we talked to him; he talked to us.' He went quiet for a moment, and then he said, 'I'd have suggested a psychiatrist, but I think I know who'll be needing psychiatric help... '

If Dave had been anyone else rather than Dave, Tyler might have offered his rather confounding explanation of what may have happened. Instead, he suggested that all things are possible and that, hopefully, everything with Greg would eventually fall into place.

It was probably at this point that the conversation should have ended, but Vincent felt obliged to leave Dave with some kind of positive assurance that things would work out and that he, Dave, was not going mad.

He said, 'There's a reason behind everything, and everything is linked or connected. It is simply a matter of finding the connections.'

There was a prolonged silence in the other end of the phone and then Dave said, 'All this bloody talk about connections... sorry, I'm going to have to go.'

And he hung up.

Tyler sat for a few moments, the telephone receiver in his hand, the fact slowly dawning on him that, in all likelihood, Greg had spoken to the detective about connections. Perhaps Greg was not as dense as he had been beginning to believe.

***

Detective Senior Constable Dave Bennett sat in his office, looking out the window. He could not stop thinking about that word *connections*. First Greg and now Tyler. Was it simply a coincidence or had Tyler been speaking with Greg?

Vincent Tyler was a strange man, but then again the entire case with the missing people and Gregory Payne was strange. He did not believe in connections or in people being in two places at the same time. He wanted the case to revert to something that resembled normality where there were normal victims and normal perpetrators and where things came together in a normal manner. He was the first to admit that the case with the missing people had not been easy; in fact it had been one of the most elusive cases he had ever had to deal with. Now it was beginning to wander off into what could only be called weird. He was not sure that he knew how to deal with it.

After about fifteen minutes, he sighed and decided that he probably needed help and that the only person who could probably give him the help he needed was Vincent Tyler. He checked the number Vincent had phoned from and dialled it.

An automated female voice answered, 'The number you dialled was incomplete or incorrect. Please check the number and dial again.'

18

Evans was extremely confused. He had believed all along that it was simply a matter of finding the person who had abducted Sandra and then everything would fall into place. He had been certain that the same person had been involved in all five disappearances, though whether or not the missing people were still alive he could not say for sure. He had been hoping that such was the case, but hope was so elusive, and there was no guarantee that everything would have a positive ending.

That was the way he had felt before Doug had caught sight of Shane on the road in the dark, and before Greg had turned up, knowing nothing about what had been going on for the last six months, believing that Sandra was at home and not missing at all.

Evans had seen Greg when he visited the office, claiming absolutely no knowledge of a missing-person's case involving his wife. The visit was made while Greg was supposedly lying in a hospital bed somewhere in Sydney. Moreover, Doug had told him that when he and Greg called in on Senior Constable Bennett, Greg had had no idea who he was. According to what Greg had said at the time, he had never seen him before.

Evans liked things to be straightforward, but this was more like something out of a science-fiction novel.

Although he had initially been focused on finding the perpetrator, he now began to think more about finding Shane. Perhaps Shane was the key, and if Doug had seen him walking around the town there was a possibility that he was still close by. Find Shane and everything would solve itself, even the mystery surrounding Greg.

It sounded simple when he thought about it, sitting in the pub, a beer in his hand; it was not so simple when he began to think where to start and how to go about finding him.

He knew that Bennett and the other police officers had trawled the town, looking for Shane, and it was highly unlikely that he, Evans, would be able to discover something that the very disciplined police department had not been able to find. Of course, the obvious place to begin had to be the place where Shane had lived. But it was five years since he had lived there, and Shane had only been renting. His few items of furniture and other personal possessions had been put into storage, and the house was now home to a family with two or three small children. Evans knew where the house was. It was a couple of streets away from where he was living, and he had once walked past, simply out of interest. From what he had been able to see, there was absolutely no indication that Shane had ever lived there.

Evans remembered standing at the fence and looking up the side of the house to the backyard where a woman had been hanging clothes on a line stretched between two trees. She had noticed him and smiled and then, probably thinking that he was looking for her, had left her washing and walked towards the fence.

Evans had immediately apologized and said that he believed Shane Lachlan had once lived in the house. A friend of a friend, he added.

The woman had shown no sign of knowing who Shane Lachlan was. She and her family had moved to the town only a year ago; however, now she came to think about it, she may have heard something about a man who had once lived in the house, a man who had later disappeared. Perhaps that was the Shane Lachlan he was looking for?

Now, sitting in the pub, Evans thought about Shane (whom he had never met), his house and the fact that the police had not been able to find anything that linked what Doug had seen that night with a physical, warm-blooded Shane. Evans guessed that it was more than possible that Shane did not want to be found, though why he did not want to be found was anyone's guess.

Also, Shane was walking away from the town when Doug claimed to have seen him. It was most unlikely that he was still in the town: he was somewhere else.

Evans ordered another beer and settled himself down to think about that *somewhere else*. What was beyond the town and where was Shane headed when Doug saw him? Where would *he* have gone if he had been Shane?

The road was the one that ran south-west out of town, past Shane's track. Evans felt that the track and the ridge were at the centre of the whole mystery; he had thought that all along, and now it seemed as though that was where Shane had been heading.

He needed to check it out for himself, even though he had no idea what he was looking for. He looked at his watch: it was getting late. Tomorrow was Saturday. He would drive out to Shane's track and then he would have a look around.

Like Greg had done.

Like Doug had done.

Evans tried to ignore a barrage of very uncomfortable

feelings that were all trying to tell him that it was really not a very good idea.

***

The next morning dawned cold but sunny, and for the end of June it looked as though the day would be reasonably pleasant. Evans managed to leave home well before eight. He drove to Shane's track, but instead of parking on the side of the main road he drove in along the track until he found a flat area adjacent to the track and completely screened from the road.

He thought it best not to take any chances.

He was still not at all happy about physically exploring the track, but he had decided that there was really no other alternative. He checked his backpack: water, compass, a hastily drawn map of the track and the area along the ridge, his mobile phone, a pen, an apple, a couple of sandwiches, a small first-aid kit...

Initially the track was reasonably easy to navigate. There were admittedly a number of ascents and descents, but the undergrowth around the actual track was either sparse or unobstructive, and the surface, while sandy, was quite firm. He followed a couple of cross tracks until they petered out into thick bush when he had no other option than to return to the main track. He had been hoping that one of the smaller tracks might have revealed something of interest, but it was becoming more and more obvious that he was going to have to follow the track all the way to the ridge.

When he reached the ridge, he had to decide whether he would continue out along the ridge or whether he would follow the smaller track downwards past the hut. He found it difficult to decide, especially the more he thought about Doug's very unpleasant experience. After about five minutes of toing and froing he decided to continue out along the ridge. He remembered that that had been Doug's intention from the beginning and that it had only been the storm that had caused him to change his mind.

It was a perfect day. Everything glistened clean and bright in the sunshine, white cockatoos screeched overhead while smaller birds flitted in and out of the vegetation lining the track. When he reached the lookout, he took a rest, gazing out over the plains below, admiring the view.

He drank some water and ate his apple. So far he had found absolutely nothing that might give some indication as to what might have happened to Shane. He decided that he would continue out along the ridge for at least another kilometre; if he had still not found anything, he would retrace his steps and then take the track down to the hut.

From where he was sitting, he could see the track wending down the side of the ridge towards the hut, but he could not see the hut itself. He returned his water bottle to his pack and was about to continue along the track when a movement on the track caught his eye. He lowered himself once more into a seated position, making sure that he was well hidden behind some vegetation.

He focused on the movement and decided that it had to be a man. After a couple of minutes, the first man was joined by a second, and the two of them began to make their way up the track. Evans was thankful that he had opted for the ridge and not for the hut. He decided, however, that he should probably stay where he was until he was quite sure where the two men were going. He settled himself into the middle of the vegetation and kept his eyes trained on the track; hopefully, the men were on their way back to the main road and not along the ridge.

***

On Monday morning, Doug looked around the office and wondered why Evans was not at his desk. No one knew anything, and Doug wondered whether he may have been taken ill. He phoned him on both his landline and his mobile, but there was no answer. For some unexplained reason, he felt quite concerned.

At lunch time, when there was still no sign of Evans and no phone call to say that he was ill, Doug decided to drive around to his house. Just to check.

Evans was not there, and his car was not in the garage.

The concern that had been quietly wrapping itself around Doug's stomach was beginning to tighten. This was not at all like Evans; obviously something must have happened.

He phoned Dave Bennett. Had he heard anything? Had there been an accident?

Dave had heard nothing, and Doug felt that he may be worrying for no reason at all. Perhaps Evans had spent the weekend in Canberra and for some reason had been delayed on his return.

But why had he not phoned?

For every attempt Doug made to quell his rising anxiety, there was a question lurking somewhere on the sidelines. A question that simply caused his anxiety to expand in every possible direction.

Dave made light of it and said that he would put out a request for information. Did Doug happen to have the number of Evans' car?

It was not until four that afternoon that Dave phoned Doug. Whereas he had been reasonably laid-back when Doug had contacted him earlier in the day, he now sounded both serious and dejected at the same time. He said:

'We found Evans' car; it was parked out on Shane's track.'

19

Doug's normally firm grasp on his mental faculties was beginning to slip, especially since returning from Sydney, realizing that Greg was actually still in hospital and could, therefore, not have visited the office. Then, while he was still processing this information, and before he was able to regain any kind of psychological equilibrium, Evans disappeared.

Evans' car, abandoned on the track, was a fairly certain indication, at least to Doug, that Evans had been doing some investigating of his own. Doug was aware that Evans was keen to solve the mystery and that he hoped, by so doing, to exonerate Doug from any responsibility for what may have happened to Sandra. Doug quite liked Evans: he was easy to get along with, he worked well and he had a sense of humour. Brian, on the other hand, had always been a mystery as far as Doug was concerned. He was already entrenched with Trust Us Insurance – "part of the furniture" was the expression he used – when Doug started working there some years back, but he had always kept to himself, and he did not seem to need or want other company. Occasionally he would join the others at the pub or in the lunch room, but, somehow, he always remained on the edge; he was always the person looking into the fish bowl, he was never one of the fish. Then, in late January or early February – there was far too much pushing around in Doug's head for him to be absolutely sure of dates – Brian suddenly left Trust Us. He had talked about needing a change and mentioned something about moving interstate and had asked Doug if he would mind taking Shane's dog, Alf. Doug had no idea where he was now; he had not heard anything from him since the day he left the office.

He wondered why he had been thinking of Brian when it was Evans who had disappeared?

Dave Bennett had been at the office all morning, asking questions, making notes. The forensic team had been studying the car and the track. Doug felt that the whole situation was like some déjà vu experience; all he wanted was for everyone to be found and for things to revert to normal. He was beginning to understand why Greg might have run off the rails. If things did not soon take a sharp turn for the better, he was beginning to worry that he might follow in Greg's footsteps.

Looking at Dave, Doug felt that he had aged several years since he saw him last. It was difficult to put a finger on what it was exactly, but he was drawn, and most of the time he seemed detached, possibly even depressed. Perhaps, like Greg and Doug, he was also balancing on the edge of sanity. The case, if one could possibly refer to it as just one case, had been going on for more than five years, and the police were still no closer to a solution. Doug could understand if Dave felt that he had failed.

While Doug was thinking about Dave, his thoughts took another path, sweeping him back to his last trip to Sydney, and how, after discovering that Greg was not at home and that he *really* was in hospital, he had taken the train and then a taxi to one of Sydney's biggest hospitals to visit his colleague.

Greg was obviously out of danger. He had been moved from ICU to a ward, and although he was swathed with bandages he was fully alert.

'This is well and truly beyond the call of duty,' he had said with the glimmer of a smile as Doug pulled up a chair and sat down next to the bed.

Doug had returned the smile, thinking to himself that he could hardly explain the real reason for his visit to Sydney. 'Not at all,' he said, 'I simply felt that it was about time for another trip to the big smoke.'

Looking at his friend, Doug knew straight away that there was no way that Greg could have been visiting the office, and yet he *had* been there. It had not been someone pretending to be Greg – it *was* Greg.

Greg was speaking again. 'They're talking about sending me home next week.' He must have seen the look of disbelief on Doug's face, because he added, 'I'll be staying with my sister and her husband, at least for the first few weeks.'

Doug nodded. The idea of someone in Greg's state having to fend for himself in an empty house was just too awful to contemplate. At least this way he would have someone looking after him.

Now, when he looked back on it all, Doug wondered if the conversation had been too superficial: Greg had little or no memory of the accident, and Doug did not feel that it was the time to talk about work-related matters. Nor had he wanted to discuss anything that Greg might have found confronting. After fifteen minutes a new visitor arrived, placing his maroon suitcase carefully next to the wall, and Doug left, wishing Greg a speedy recovery, promising to keep in touch.

It was when Doug arrived back in the town that he

began to fall apart. There were too many questions and not enough answers. He decided that he definitely needed to get away for a while, to some place where he could perhaps forget about missing people and people who seemed to be in two places at the same time.

***

In spite of the layer of gloom that had settled over the entire case, Dave was suddenly rewarded with a breakthrough. The forensic team was able to confirm that there had been at least two people in the hut sometime over the past few days. The footprints found in and around the hut were then picked up along the track leading away from the hut and up towards the ridge. They were eventually lost, but were found further along the ridge, together with a third set of footprints. The new set was traced back all the way to Evans' car.

Dave had studied the patterns the footprints had made in the sandy soil on the ridge, trying to get some idea of what might have happened there. He assumed from the size of the footprints that they all belonged to men, but whether the men knew each other and met as friends, or whether there had been some kind of scuffle was difficult to say. The tracker brought in to help trace the footprints said that there was a good chance that they were made at different times, but he agreed that all three people had obviously been both on the track and on the ridge itself. As well as the footprints, they found a couple of cigarette butts, and everyone Dave asked was adamant that Evans did not smoke.

The entire area was cordoned off, and Dave insisted that every centimetre should be analysed and tested. He was sick and tired of going around in circles and constantly coming up against brick walls. There had to be something, however small or incongruous, that would point him in the right direction.

Dave desperately wanted to be pointed in the right direction.

However, with the breakthrough, Dave was actually beginning to resemble his old self. He had suspected all along that there was someone else involved in the disappearances, and now he felt that he might have the evidence. He was one hundred percent certain that Evans' disappearance was linked to the disappearance of the five other people. Now all he had to do was to find the perpetrator or the perpetrators.

***

The breakthrough in the case came only a couple of days after Dave had phoned Vincent a second time. He had been feeling desperate, and his thoughts kept returning to the growing realization that the only person who might be able to help him was Vincent Tyler. Although part of his mind was clinging to the possibility that Tyler might be the key to the whole thing, a larger part of his mind was warning him against becoming too involved with, and dependent on, someone who felt that isolating the connections was the only way of solving a crime. Dave had to admit to himself that it felt insane, but there was nothing else. There was no real Plan B, and Plan A had been failing miserably. Dave had reached a point where he was prepared to try anything.

Then he remembered that when he last tried to call Tyler he had received an incorrect-number message.

Eventually, Dave decided that the worst that could happen was that he would get the same message, and

156

he dialled the number, telling himself that, this time, Tyler would answer the phone.

And he did.

'Vincent Tyler here.'

Dave had been so taken aback that everything he had thought to say simply evaporated.

'Hello! Tyler here.' The voice sounded slightly stressed, annoyed even.

Dave guessed that if he did not answer soon Tyler would hang up. He said, 'Mr Tyler? It's Dave Bennett, Senior Constable... '

Tyler's voice changed. He sounded pleased that Dave had phoned him. After the initial greetings, Dave said, 'I tried to phone you a while back, but I received an incorrect-number message. I was a bit reluctant to phone again, but it was the only number I had-'

Vincent Tyler interrupted, saying, 'And that *is* my number.' He was quiet for a moment and then continued, 'You must ask yourself, Bennett: what were you actually hoping for when you phoned me that first time? Did you *really* want me to answer? Was there some part of you hoping that I would *not* answer?'

'But-'

'We create our realities, Senior Constable Bennett.'

Dave grimaced at the phone, wondering if he had made the right decision after all. He said, 'When we last talked, before I hung up... ' He paused and then he continued, 'you said something about connections. I was given the feeling that you might possibly have an answer to what has happened, or at least a suggestion... even if you could put us on the right track, it would be much appreciated.'

Vincent Tyler did not answer straight away, and Dave began to worry that perhaps he had overstepped some kind of boundary.

He added, 'Of course, I may have misunderstood; perhaps no one has the answer.'

Tyler spoke suddenly. 'Everything is connected. We can't do or say anything without it affecting something or someone. I don't have all the information about these missing people, but the fact that they have all gone missing is one important connection, tying them all together. There must be other connections as well; it is just a matter of finding them.'

The voice on the end of the phone went quiet for a moment, and then Tyler continued, 'Do you remember those murders south of Sydney some years back? They were all young people; they were all murdered in the same forest; and they were all backpackers. Beyond all those obvious connections, they were all hitch-hiking; it was this umbrella connection that caused them to be murdered.'

While Dave was saying that he remembered, he was wondering what on earth the umbrella connection could be in the case he was trying to solve. Was it the track, or was it something else?

Vincent was talking again, 'Look at each person separately and then look at the connections between them. Who were they? Why were they on the track? Where were they going? There are lines running between these people; the thickest one at the moment is that they are all missing. It is important to isolate these lines, no matter how thin or how faint they might be.'

Dave was not sure if Tyler was making any sense, but it was worth a try. He thanked him and then he ended the call.

***

Working along the top of the ridge was a frustrating and time-consuming activity. Sand was examined for footprints; stones were scrutinized before a decision could be made as to whether or not they had been moved; bushes were inspected for broken branches, a sure sign that someone had passed that way. Finally, a police dog was brought in, and after some moments of uncertainty, while it nosed around in the bushes near the track, it lifted its head and headed down the side of the ridge away from the track, its handler only metres behind.

The dog had obviously picked up a scent, and the police who were turning over stones and comparing footprints stopped work and watched the dog rush down the side of the ridge. There was no actual track, and the incline was quite steep, but the dog seemed to know where it was going. The handler was joined by two of the men who had been studying footprints, and the three men scrambled down the side of the ridge, grabbing hold of bushes and rocks to stop themselves from slipping.

After about five minutes, the dog and the men vanished from view beneath a rock overhang, and the men up on top of the ridge were left wondering as to whether this was what they had been looking forward to for years or whether it was simply a wild-goose chase. Was the answer to the missing people somewhere down there along the side of the ridge?

Dave watched the dog until it disappeared, a multitude of thoughts running through his head. He did not dare hope that, after so long, he could actually be standing at the very edge of some kind of quantum leap forward. He stepped off the ridge and, pushing his way through the thick undergrowth, carefully followed the three men and the dog. At the rock overhang, he lowered himself past the obstruction and caught sight of the men clustered together a little below him and further to his right.

Dave's heart began to beat faster. Had they actually discovered something? Is this where it all ended?

20

Greg was now ensconced at his sister's home. With his electric wheelchair, he was able to move between his bedroom and the living areas of the house without too much problem; he could even wheel himself out on to the back veranda, which overlooked a stretch of untamed bushland. His injuries were slowly healing, and he was looking forward to soon being able to move around without any help and, eventually, to be able to return home. He loved his sister, he got along well with his brother-in-law, but he needed his independence.

Sitting out on the back veranda, a blanket wrapped around him, he had plenty of time to think. He tried not to dwell on his fall and what may have caused it, but he was completely unable to stop his thoughts from zooming in on Vincent Tyler and his suggestion that he should be isolating the connections.

He also thought about Vincent's visit while he was in hospital.

Greg had not been expecting Doug to turn up at the hospital, and he had certainly not expected Tyler to visit him. He remembered how the older man had entered the ward just as Doug was preparing to leave. He also remembered thinking that, for some unexplained reason, he really wanted Doug to stay; he did not want to be left alone with Tyler.

As Doug left, Tyler sat down, asking Greg how he was feeling. Then he paused a moment and said that he had actually seen him fall.

Greg was amazed, and he wondered what Tyler had been doing on the platform. Had he been following him or had his being there at that particular moment simply been a coincidence?

'It was a really bad fall,' Tyler continued, 'it is quite unbelievable that you survived.'

Greg replied that he could not remember anything at all from the moment he stepped on to the escalator. In many ways he felt that it was fortunate that his memory had chosen to seal off such awful images; he really doubted that he could have coped had his head been full of escalator steps and downward plunges. He disliked heights at the best of times, and the prospect of reliving such a terrifying, uncontrolled descent over and over again would have been too much to contemplate.

Tyler was still talking. 'You were thrown from one step to the next, and then about halfway down you did a sort of half somersault, and you finally landed on your head. It was terrible to watch; it must have been-'

Greg shuddered. He had heard enough. He interrupted Tyler, 'Thank God I can't remember anything.'

Tyler looked at Greg's bandages. 'Many broken bones?' he asked.

'Arm broken in two places, broken leg, broken ankle, two dislocated shoulders, a fractured skull... and, as you can see, plenty of cuts and bruises.'

Tyler grimaced and shook his head but said nothing.

Greg continued, 'It was the skull fracture that caused most concern... but that's all behind me now.' Then he added, 'It was kind of you- '

'Not really,' said Tyler, anticipating what Greg was

about to say. 'We seem to be bumping into each other; it is almost as though there is- '

'A connection?' Greg managed a weak smile. 'Yes, perhaps we do have some kind of connection, though why, I'd have absolutely no idea.'

Vincent did not answer straight away, but he did return Greg's smile. After a few moments, he said, 'How are you going with the other connections?'

Greg shook his head. 'I must admit, it's all a bit beyond me. I did find connections between some of the missing people but not all of them. To be honest, I feel as though I am groping around in the dark.'

Tyler said, 'Perhaps it is because you are looking for connections in the wrong places?'

'That's possible,' replied Greg. 'but, as I said, it's all a bit beyond me.'

The older man shrugged. 'I don't have all the facts; I'm just saying what *I'd* do in the situation. There are always threads running in all directions, nothing exists on its own; nothing happens without affecting something else. As I said to you before: isolate these threads and perhaps they will lead you to the solution. Also, keep in mind that nothing in this world is final and absolute: everything is on its way somewhere else; all connections are merely a change of direction. No one can stop this from happening; it is a fact of life.'

The conversation gradually changed to more superficial things, and after about fifteen minutes Tyler left, though not before wishing Greg a quick return to full health.

Now, on the veranda, the winter sun sketching bright, cold lines across the expanse of bush in front of him, Greg's thoughts returned to the hospital and moved around what Tyler had said about *connections* and how each connection was somehow like a nodule, signifying a change of path. He could not help but think of a diagram he had seen of the brain with its network of lines all anchored to small node-like points. He was able to understand the bit about paths or threads joining everything, but he could not work out how it might be possible to find those threads, especially when they stretched back over so many years and so many people.

Greg knew that the number of people missing had increased from five to six, and he was even more certain that no one was even vaguely in control. As far as he could see, everything was threatening to implode or explode or do something that was equally as disastrous. In spite of Tyler's insistence on connections, there did not seem to be any.

While he was thinking about how hopeless everything was, his eye was caught by some bright yellow-orange spiky flowers nestled between dark green leaves. The flowers were attractive and Greg appreciated their presence in what was otherwise a green midwinter landscape. There was a very slight breeze, and the flowers occasionally swayed, creating different patterns. As Greg looked, the yellows and the oranges blurred and merged, taking on other tones and other highlights. The flowers became birds, sitting on the branch. Greg's brain knew that he was looking at flowers, but bit by bit he became less certain, and although it was completely ridiculous he was prepared to accept that he could actually be looking at birds.

Yellow birds and dark green leaves.

Different realities.

Things did not have to appear the same to everyone all the time or even part of the time. His memory of what had happened in January would always remain *his* memory shaped by his experiences and by who he was. For the umpteenth time, he went over the couple of days he had spent with Sandra in the town way back in January. He had already dissected every move, every conversation, every decision, but he did it once again, trying to pretend that he was someone else, someone looking in from the outside. There was an uncomfortable thought or distorted image on the very edge of his memory, attempting to catch his attention. He had a very strong feeling that it may have had something to do with Sandra, but for some reason he veered away from it, grabbing on to all the things he knew or thought he knew.

He decided that there were so many different ways of looking at the same thing. His head was beginning to ache from the overabundance of thoughts and possible scenarios, and yet still nothing cried out to him, saying emphatically, 'This is what happened.'

He had moved into the equation of missing people when he and Sandra visited the town in January; Shane had moved into it when he drove in on the track...

He was on the point of giving up when a new thought appeared from nowhere. At first it was no more than a small speck on the horizon, but it quickly became larger, and soon it filled his whole head. Everyone had been pulled into this case from somewhere else. Somewhere, way out on some edge, each of the people involved had his or her own life, own job, own friends... the connections were all out there on the edge. There were not necessarily any connections at the centre of the web, which is where Greg placed the track. All these people arrived at the centre burdened with what might have been going on in their lives out on the edge, the point that was furthest from the track and furthest from each other.

Greg took a deep breath, and then to no one in particular he muttered, 'Of course, there doesn't have to be any kind of connection between each of the missing people and the track. That everyone went missing on or near the track may not be at all important – or not as important as we've been imagining. What *is* important is what was going on in these people's lives before they actually reached the track. Perhaps the track itself is completely insignificant.'

He picked up his mobile phone, thinking that he would call Vincent Tyler, but, realizing that he did not have Tyler's number, he dialled Dave Bennett's number instead.

***

Dave sat with the telephone in his hand long after Greg had finished talking. On the one hand he was relieved that Greg actually knew who he was – it was as though the bizarre meeting when Greg had claimed no knowledge of him had never taken place – but on the other hand he was not sure whether he was prepared to accept Greg's idea or not. Dave knew that he and his team had examined what each of the missing people had been doing in their lives before they went missing, but, thinking about it, there was a possibility that they did not dig deep enough. Perhaps there were other things going on about which they knew absolutely nothing, things that were hidden deep beneath the surface, things that eventually caused each of the six people to disappear in one way or another. Perhaps some of them actually wanted to disappear and the track had simply become a kind of scapegoat. Everyone had been concentrating on the track as the one thing linking all the disappearances – and in a way this was correct – but it may have blinkered everyone as to what had really happened.

He put down the phone and walked to the window. They had been looking at the track as something pulling everything together into a combined case with the same perpetrator (or perpetrators), but if they were to accept Greg's idea then, in a way, they would be back at square one. Dave closed his eyes and tried to get his head around a new set of possibilities.

He had always believed that it was a case of people being in the wrong place at the wrong time, and he was reluctant to let go the idea of a common perpetrator. Greg's idea was original, but whether or not it held the answer to the mystery Dave really had no idea. If it turned out that Greg was right, then these people would most probably have vanished even if they had never come in contact with the track.

He turned away from the window, opened the filing cabinet, took out the files for the six missing people and placed them on his desk. He decided that it could be worthwhile concentrating on all those things at the end of each thread and, for a moment at least, avoid looking for any kind of connection at the centre.

He opened Evans' file, thinking back to the search on the ridge. He flicked through the pages rereading paragraphs, trying to pinpoint something, anything, that might explain why Evans had disappeared without a trace.

As he read, he remembered scrambling down the side of the ridge and reaching the three men who had gone down before him. The dog had been sitting to one side, its eyes fixed on its handler.

Dave had asked the men if they had found anything, and one of them pointed to a barely perceptible track winding along the side of the ridge to the right. He could hear water, and he guessed that further along there was probably a creek and possibly a waterfall.

One of the men said, 'It's almost certain that they went that way.'

Dave thought: There was nothing saying that Evans was part of the 'they,' and in spite of all the conscientious searching and forensic examination the 'they' could well be a couple of innocent bushwalkers.

He said, 'We'll need to check it out.'

Dave sighed audibly and continued looking at the papers in Evans' folder, hoping that something might jump out at him and give him a clue as to what might have happened. He remembered that Evans was initially from Queensland, and perhaps Evans' time in Queensland could shed some light on the far end of *his* thread. Dave knew that the information had been noted, but as far as he knew no one had considered it of any great importance.

He pulled out the relevant document and read that prior to leaving Queensland Evans had worked for a small construction company in Brisbane. When a large amount of money went missing, the finger had been pointed at Evans: he was, after all, the accounts manager. Although an in-depth investigation revealed that there was absolutely nothing to tie Evans to the missing money, the damage had already been done. Peeved that he had been under suspicion for something that he had not done, Evans immediately severed ties with the company, the city and the state.

Dave stretched his legs and put his hands behind his head. He was fully prepared to believe that Evans was completely innocent, but there was a chance that he may have known who took the money, and perhaps the person who took the money knew that Evans knew. It was an extremely long shot, but Dave had to begin somewhere, so he checked the name of the construction company and dialled the number.

21

Evans was not at all sure that he had done the right thing in coming out to the track on his own; he probably should have told someone what he was doing or at least he should have left a note. If anything were to happen to him then... but he decided that he did not want to think about such things. He had to remain positive and focused. To remain focused meant that he had to rid himself of all negative thoughts.

He was sitting up on the ridge, watching the two men below leave the hut and then walk slowly up the track. He was desperately hoping that they would continue along the track to the road, but then they turned off and began to walk towards him along the ridge. It was when they were only metres away that he began to wonder whether or not he actually knew one of them. Holding his breath, he very cautiously parted a couple of the branches of the bush, behind which he was hiding, and saw, to his amazement, that one of the men was Brian.

He had never had a lot to do with Brian, who had left the company way back at the beginning of the year, but Evans felt that he could regard him, if not as a friend at least as an acquaintance. He did not recognize the man with him, but obviously he was a friend of Brian's.

Evans was about to stand up and push his way out on to the track when something stopped him. He was almost sure that he heard Brian call the other man *Shane*, and if the man with Brian was actually Shane then something very weird was going on. He remembered being with Brian when they had all been talking about Shane, and Brian had not given any indication then that Shane was not missing. Or was it that he was missing then, but he was not missing now? Evans really did not know what to think, but a strong sense of self-preservation kept him huddled behind the bushes.

Brian and the man, who Evans now knew was Shane, continued along the track, and twenty metres further on from where Evans was hiding they turned off to the left and clambered down the side of the ridge. Evans was able to see the two men disappear over the edge, but he knew that if he wanted to see where they were going he would have to follow them.

Everything that was in any way logical was telling him to return to the car. Following Brian and Shane was not going to solve anything; it could, in fact, put him in a lot of danger. But Evans was curious, and ignoring everything that was telling him to do exactly the opposite, he cautiously walked along the track and, at the point where he saw the two men disappear, began the steep descent down from the ridge.

He could not see either of the men, but he expected that they were not that far in front of him. The undergrowth was thick, which was to his advantage, but the badly designated track was extremely steep. After negotiating a rocky overhang, the barely noticeable path flattened out somewhat and followed the side of the ridge. Evans suspected that he was now moving parallel to the track on the top of the ridge but some fifty metres lower down.

He could hear sounds of falling water, and he very

soon broke through a maze of tall, prickly bushes to see a small creek in front of him. The creek obviously originated somewhere further up on the ridge, and some metres beyond Evans, on his left, it created a waterfall as it fell down the steepest part of the escarpment.

Halfway up the ridge on his right, he could see Shane and Evans. They were actually wading in the creek and looked as they were studying something. Every now and then, one of them would bend down and pick up what seemed to be small stones, and they would then both converse quietly for a few minutes before moving further up the creek, away from the waterfall, closer to the top of the ridge.

Evans wondered what on earth they were doing.

He wanted to get a better view, but he did not want to be seen. He moved further to his left, hoping to be able to use the cover of the vegetation to see what was going on. What he did not know was that it was at just that point that the ground, covered by dense vegetation, fell away.

He took yet another step to the left, but his foot did not connect with anything solid. He felt himself slipping and sliding. The bushes he grabbed on to gave way, and within seconds he found himself plunging over the side of the ridge.

***

Shane and Brian both looked up from what they were doing. Shane asked, 'Did you hear something?

Brian peered across the creek into the undergrowth. 'Most probably a wallaby,' he said, and as if on cue three wallabies hopped across the creek and quickly disappeared.

22

When Dave phoned the company in Brisbane where Evans had worked, he merely received confirmation of what he already knew; however, he did learn that the man who had taken the money had been apprehended and that he had been in gaol for the past six months. The man had no connection at all with Evans, and Dave's theory that Evans knew more than he should have known and that he was being threatened for what he may have known dissipated before Dave even had a chance to end the call. If Evans was in trouble, it definitely had nothing to do with what had happened in Brisbane.

He sighed and returned to Evans' file. Whether or not he was hoping for some kind of enlightened awareness is difficult to say, but even after a second reading he found nothing of importance. As far as he could see, Evans was an ordinary young man who had simply gone missing. If there was foul play involved, there was absolutely nothing in the file that indicated why and or how.

Dave closed the file and returned it to the cabinet. Perhaps he needed to question Evans' work colleagues again.

***

As Dave and the other three policemen clambered through the dense undergrowth towards what they guessed was probably a creek, Dave was thinking about Evans and the phone call, and how it had not amounted to anything significant; he was also thinking that he had not yet had time to talk to anyone from Trust Us Insurance.

The dog had run on ahead, still obviously following a scent, and everyone was cautiously confident that they were heading in the right direction. After about ten minutes, they broke out of the undergrowth and in front of them was a shallow, rocky creek. Dave could see that the creek originated somewhere up on the ridge on his right, tumbling down the side of the ridge by a series of very small steps or falls. Further to his left he guessed from the sound of falling water that it then fell all the way to the flat below.

The dog was sniffing around the rocks near the creek, but Dave guessed that it may have lost the scent. After a few moments of deliberation, two of the men continued over the creek, beating a path in the direction they had all been walking, while Dave, the dog and the dog handler climbed up the creek to the ridge.

At times they had to pull themselves up over the tumble of rocks and boulders bordering the creek; at other times, their only way forward was through the creek itself, where they were forced to look for stepping stones that were not too slippery, while grabbing hold of overhanging branches, often in the nick of time, to keep themselves from falling.

It took them almost half an hour to reach the ridge,

and then they continued along the top in a southerly direction, all the time following the creek. It was difficult to know whether or not the dog had picked up the scent again, but unless they were to follow the ridge back towards the hut and the road then there was really no other direction to take.

The creek eventually widened into a large pool, beyond which towered the massive rock face that signalled the end of the ridge. The rocky outcrop, which collected water for the creek, was also riddled with caves. Dave looked up at the precipice, wondering if it somehow held the key to all his problems, and while he was looking, a man appeared from the darkness of one of the many openings.

'I think you may be looking for me,' he said. 'I'm Shane. Shane Lachlan.'

23

It was an unbelievable story. Dave doubted he would
have accepted it in a second-rate paperback novel, and
yet here he was having to admit that Shane Lachlan had
completely led them all astray, both him and the entire
police department. Now that he knew how everything
fitted together, he could understand how he had been
fooled into going down the wrong path. He had started
out with a vague idea of what might have happened, and
that had obviously been his wrong doing. Vincent's
insistence on connections was not as stupid as he had
first thought; had he concentrated more on what was
going on in Shane's life prior to his disappearance, he
might not have been so ready to jump to conclusions.

Or perhaps it would not have helped at all.

He had sat with Shane for more than an hour in the
small room at the back of the station that doubled as an
interview room. If Shane was repentant, he did not show
it. He may have been disappointed that everything had
fallen apart, but at the same time he seemed strangely
relieved that he no longer had to hide.

Dave had questioned him several times about the
other missing people, and although Shane admitted that
he remembered the two Germans and although he was
aware that other people had gone missing he insisted
that he was unable to give him any information.

Dave rewound the tape recorder and pressed the play button. After the formal introductions, he could hear himself saying, 'If you could start at the beginning...'

Shane's voice filled the room. 'I owed money. It doesn't matter why, but... well, I needed money, quickly. There was no point going to the bank, they'd never have given me a loan, and then a mate put me on to this fellow. He seemed genuine, friendly even. No paperwork, just a handshake, and the money was mine. I was desperate; I know now that I didn't think it through properly.'

In his mind's eye, Dave could see Shane leaning back in the chair, placing his hands behind his neck and then dropping them on to his knee.

'Once I'd got the money, I began straight away to worry about having to pay it back. In the beginning, the fellow said there was no rush, then after about a year, he said there'd been a change of plan and he needed the money a.s.a.p. He also insisted that the interest was much more than we'd agreed upon. And I couldn't do a damn thing about it because, you know, there was just that handshake and no paperwork.

'I did my best to keep up with the payments, but it all got completely beyond me. There wasn't enough work to make it cut even. Quite honestly, I didn't know what I was going to do... he was getting real nasty and then he gave me an ultimatum: pay up or else. From the way he said it, I didn't have to wonder what the 'or else' meant.

'Then one night when I was sitting at home, watching television, this idea came to me: I could simply disappear. I wouldn't have to disappear for ever, just long enough for people to forget about me, and then I could start all over again. Somewhere else.'

There was a loud scratching noise on the tape, and Dave remembered Shane moving the chair and resting his hands on the table.

'I thought about it for a couple of days, and I reckoned it was actually possible. Then I suggested it to Brian. You see, Brian and I are mates. We'd met in the pub years ago and we, like, hit it off straight away. Brian used to work for that insurance crowd, but he's just a normal, down-to-earth fellow. He was the only one I told about the loan. He never says much, but he listens, and he's real loyal...

'Anyway, I told Brian what I'd been thinking, and he told me that I was completely mad. He said I should be talking to you instead, and perhaps I should've listened to him, but I felt it was too much of a risk, and anyway, by that stage, I'd more or less made up my mind. I asked him if he'd help me. At first he said he wouldn't, but then he changed his mind and said that he would.'

There was a pause, and then Shane's voice again, 'Any chance of a cigarette?'

An audible click as the machine was turned off and then some background noise as it was turned on again and Shane's voice, 'Thanks. Where were we? Yes, Brian... well, he said he'd help me and then it was just a matter of me working out all the details.'

'Brian reckoned that I should just up and disappear from the town, travel north into Queensland or even west, but as I explained to him it would never have worked. The whole bloody country would've been out looking for me, reports going this way and that way; it would've only been a matter of time 'til someone somewhere stumbled over me. I just couldn't take the risk.

'No, I decided that if I was going to disappear, I had to do it properly. People had to believe I was dead. Once I was tagged as "Missing, presumed dead" then people would stop looking for me, especially the fellow I owed money. People don't go 'round looking for dead people, do they? They accept that the person's dead, and then they move on to other things. This is what I wanted: I wanted to be forgotten and I wanted everyone to start thinking about other things. My plan was to wait until the fuss had died down, and then, with a few changes to my appearance and a new name, I intended to move interstate, using the back roads and avoiding towns. I knew that when I reached Queensland, I could pick up work outback. Eventually I might have even gone west and started a new life... '

Dave heard his own voice break into the recording, 'So, what went wrong?'

'Nothing and everything. In the beginning, everything went just as I had planned. I know the ridge like the back of my hand, and I knew that there were a lot of caves in the south... '

Dave thought: Of course, that was where they had found him.

'Anyway, during the weeks before I disappeared, I moved some stuff up there: you know, tinned stuff, sleeping bag, blankets, extra clothes... there's one cave there, it's not awfully big, and you can only get to it through the roof of one of the other caves. If you don't know where the opening is, you'd never find it, not in a million years.'

Dave remembered that they had done a quick search of the caves, after Shane disappeared and again after Sandra had disappeared, but they had found nothing. They had not been expecting to find anything there. As far as they were concerned, the search area had to radiate out from the hut, and the caves were a long way from the hut. Beyond the caves, the ridge came to a very abrupt and particularly steep end. If Shane, and, in fact, any of the missing people, had been abducted, as was the general assumption, then the only way off the ridge and out of the area was to follow the track down via the hut, or to return to the main road.

'The cave was high up, and there was a small opening, almost a window, in the side, and I had a view all the way back down the ridge. When you were first looking for me, I just sat there and watched; if you'd come any closer, I'd have simply moved deeper into the caves.

The scratching noise was heard again as Shane moved his chair closer to the table.

'Anyway, the day I disappeared, I drove in on the track, but you know that... ' He gave a short, uncertain laugh before continuing. 'The very worst thing was leaving Alf. I'd have done anything to have taken Alf with me, but then it would have looked suspicious. He's a good dog, Alf. When I told him to stay, he stayed, even though he probably wanted to follow me. I spent several hours walking in circles around the area, laying false trails just in case you decided to use dogs. I had a change of clothes and boots, some stuff that Brian had picked up at the Salvo's and left near the hut a couple of days earlier. That way they had none of my smell on them. Sometime around midnight, I changed clothes, wrapped my clothes in the plastic bag the new clothes had been in and dropped the parcel down a deep cleft between two rocks beyond the hut. If the clothes were to be found, which I very much doubted, then it wouldn't have mattered that much, it would have just confirmed that something had happened to me.

'By this time I was pretty done in, but I knew that I had to get out of the area and up to the caves. I took the most roundabout route I could take and then I waded through the dam... '

There was a long pause at this point, and Dave guessed that Shane was reliving the discomfort, even the horror, of wading through black, cold water in the middle of the night.

'Not the best thing I've ever done, but I had dry clothes in the cave.'

Once again, Dave heard his own voice, 'None of this can have been easy in the dark.'

He remembered Shane's smile as he said, 'Head lamp, and, as I said before, I know the area– '

Dave finished the sentence, '... like the back of your hand.'

After a very short pause, Shane's voice continued, 'I stayed up there in the caves for several weeks. Brian came out once with extra food and to let me know that he was looking after Alf. He, Brian that is, had to be real careful no one was following him. Then after about a month, he turned up one evening and told me that the search on the ridge had been wound back and that you were concentrating on some of the surrounding towns. He also told me about the memorial service... ' Shane's voice faded to silence. There was a short spate of coughing and then Shane was talking again.

'Even with my new beard and long hair, I didn't feel safe enough to move on yet, and decided to wait for at least another month, but the fact that the police were no longer searching the ridge meant that I had a bit more freedom. I just had to pick my times... also I had to have eyes in the back of my head.

'Some days I took a walk back along the ridge, and occasionally, if I could be sure that there was no one around, I walked down to the hut. It was on one of these visits to the hut that my plans took a very definite change of direction... ' He was quiet for a moment, and then he said, 'Looking back on it, I wonder if it had perhaps been better if I'd stuck to my original idea and simply moved interstate.'

Dave sighed as he turned off the tape recorder. He could not agree more with Shane, but he knew that most people, including himself, were usually much wiser in hindsight than they were in that moment of making a decision.

24

Vincent Tyler had taken a flight to the town soon after Detective Senior Constable Bennett had phoned him. Initially he was somewhat surprised that Bennett would have contacted him, but the more he thought about it he decided that perhaps it did make sense, in a strange sort of way. For some reason everything had been pulling him back to his grandfather's hut, the track and the missing people. From the tiny airport, he took a taxi direct to the police station. Bennett met him in the reception.

'Not exactly what we had expected,' said Tyler as he followed Dave into his office. 'I'm still trying to come to terms with what it all means. For me and for everyone else. But, of course, you'll have to fill me in; there are still a lot of gaps... '

Dave gestured Tyler to a chair and then he sat down opposite him. 'I'd have to agree,' he said, 'both in regards to what it means and the gaps.' Since accepting Tyler's idea about connections, Dave's respect for the man had increased markedly. He had done some research into Tyler's background – beyond his connection with Gordon Parrish – and he had to admit to himself that he was impressed. He was able to see that there was a certain benefit in being able to discuss ideas with such a person – ideas about people who had vanished without a trace.

Tyler rested his hand on his suitcase, standing beside

183

his chair. 'So... ?'

Dave took a deep breath and then he gave Vincent a brief summary of what Shane had told him about his need to disappear, and how he had orchestrated the whole thing. He mentioned the help that Shane had received from Brian, and how Brian had eventually, after several years, moved up to the ridge to be on hand twenty-four seven. Then he told Vincent about Shane's visit to the hut.

It had been been an evening at the end of summer when Shane had visited the hut. He had been hiding up on the ridge for about six weeks, and he was almost ready to put the second part of his plan into action and move interstate. He was expecting to see Brian again in two days' time, and, all going well, Brian had offered to drive him to a highway fifty kilometres further west, from where he would have picked up a lift going north.

The hut was much the same as it had always been. Like Doug and a number of other locals, Shane had occasionally used the hut if he was trapped on the ridge by bad weather. He liked the hut; it was bare and wind-swept, but it had a friendly feel about it.

He looked around the inside of the hut and then, not really expecting to find anything but having plenty of time on his hands, he wandered back outside. On the far side of the hut there was a small lean-to shed. It was little more than one metre high and not much more than that in breadth, but it was all but hidden by the encroaching undergrowth. Only someone actually look-ing for it or, as in Shane's situation, someone with loads of spare time, would notice that it was even there. As Shane pulled apart the bushes and looked at the solid, padlocked door, he had a feeling that this was not just any shed and that whatever was in that shed was about to send his life in a direction he had not dared contemplate.

Without the proper tools, it took him a while to break the padlock, but time and rust were on his side. With the lock finally broken, he pushed away the creepers and scrub and opened the door.

Inside there were a number of old tools – a mattock, a spade, an axe, a hoe – and a couple of rusty tin buckets. Shane was on the point of closing the shed again, admittedly with some disappointment, when it occurred to him that the width of the shed on the outside was more than it was on the inside. When he investigated he found a false wall that could be lifted out with some effort, and behind this wall a space of about twenty-five or thirty centimetres.

In the small space there were gold fossicking tools: a pan, a pick, a shovel and a sledge hammer. Hanging from a nail in the far wall, there was a thin, grey-blue exercise book. Shane carefully removed the book and opened it. The book was extremely dusty, and the pages misshapen and discoloured, but he was able to make out the many rows of figures, some of which had been crossed out. Towards the centre of the book there were a number of hand-drawn maps and diagrams. Shane immediately recognized the maps as maps of the ridge, and each one had at least one cross with a name scrawled next to it. The names, *Far Rise* and *No Worries*, had obviously been made up by the person who had drawn the map, probably the old hermit who had lived in the hut, but the crosses had to be places where gold had been discovered.

At this point of the narration, Vincent Tyler nodded his head, but did not say anything. Things began to make sense: he could now understand why his grandfather had

remained on the ridge for so long; he was also begin-
ning to understand why he had been murdered.

Shane was trying to work out whether or not he had discovered anything worthwhile when his eye fell on a tin box in the corner of the shed. When he opened it, he found, wrapped in a piece of stained and dirty cotton, a handful of small gold nuggets. He guessed the weight to be around four hundred grams, which converted to cash would have been somewhere in the vicinity of twenty thousand dollars.

He could pay off his debt, and he would have money over. He would not have to move interstate at all. He could devise some kind of story about falling over and hitting his head on a rock just after he had stepped out of his truck. Perhaps he could say that he ended up with amnesia and, not knowing what he was doing, he had walked back to the road and hitched a ride to Melbourne. There were lots of possibilities; he would have to give it some thought.

On the other hand, he could take the tools and study the maps. If the hermit had been able to find gold, then perhaps he could find it as well. Why should he be content with twenty thousand when it might be possible to double it or even triple it.

Shane squatted next to the shed, the gold still in his hand. Whether he fully understood it or not, whatever he finally decided was going to have a major impact on the rest of his life.

***

While Vincent had been listening to Dave Bennett, his mind had been grappling with the fact that Shane knew absolutely nothing about the other people who had gone missing. On one level, it appeared that everyone had vanished on the track, but perhaps that was not the case at all. Vincent could see that the track had confused everyone. Dave had told him about Greg's idea that the connections might all be at the edge and not at the centre. The idea made a lot of sense to Vincent, and he was impressed that Greg had reached such a conclusion. But something about Greg was worrying him.

It concerned Greg, but it also concerned Sandra.

Sitting in his hotel room after his afternoon meeting with Bennett, Vincent was trying to piece together everything he knew. He could agree with Greg that the connections between each person and his or her disappearance probably had more to do with the far end of each thread than where they met the track at the centre, but what was going on in Sandra's life that would have caused her to disappear? From his very few talks with Greg, he had the idea that there was nothing in Sandra's life that could possibly have equated with a disappearance. On the other hand, he had noticed that Greg never mentioned her any more; something that he felt was both strange and disconcerting.

Perhaps there were things about Sandra and Greg's relationship that had never been fully investigated; perhaps everyone simply assumed that it was a normal relationship.

Tyler thought for a moment, and even though it was well after hours he phoned Bennett's mobile. 'Just a thought,' he said, after he had apologized for phoning so late. 'I could be barking up the wrong tree, but I can't stop thinking about Greg's relationship with his wife; I'm wondering if it was all that it was made out to be. If I were you I'd phone his sister; perhaps she knows something that we don't.'

Half an hour later Bennett phoned him back. 'You were right,' he said. 'Sandra was intending to leave Greg. She had met someone else.'

25

In the end, Shane made the decision to remain on the ridge and fossick for gold. The chance of substantially increasing the gold he had already found was just too much for him to ignore. He was already missing, and people had stopped looking for him. It was the ideal situation, and he felt he should not waste it. He had no pangs of conscience about removing the gold he had found in the old hermit's hut. From what he knew the man was a loner, without relatives, and as far as Shane was concerned the gold was the property of whoever happened to find it. In this case, Shane.

For the next months, Shane systematically worked his way though several of Gordon's maps. He would spend several weeks fossicking in one spot, and then he would move on to another spot. Most of the gold was alluvial, being washed down by several creeks that flowed across the ridge. Shane suspected that there could be a seam of gold running through the ridge, but without a metal detector it was almost impossible to prove one way or the other.

Brian had been extremely opposed to Shane's decision to remain on the ridge and look for gold; he felt that he should be content with what he had already found. However, when he realized that Shane had made up his mind, and when Shane offered him a percentage for being the man on the outside, Brian went along with the decision. He continued to make food drops every few weeks, and when Shane needed something, like a metal detector or wet-weather gear, he would drive to Canberra, or one of the bigger towns further south, and return with whatever it was that Shane had ordered. On a few occasions, Brian even stayed overnight, helping Shane as he worked his way down through the thick sand in an icy-cold creek, or as he patiently moved along specific parts of the ridge with his metal detector.

After a year and a half, Shane had added almost an extra two hundred grams of gold to the original four hundred. It was slow work, with many disappointments, but Shane saw no reason to give up. Not yet.

One morning, at the beginning of the second winter of his disappearance, Shane had taken a walk along the ridge back towards the hut. The hut had become a fixture in his life, offering him a welcome escape from his cave.

No one had been near the ridge for weeks, and he was not as cautious as he normally would have been. He was reasonably pleased with how things were going, even if the very primitive, isolated lifestyle had its obvious drawbacks: there were many times when he found himself contemplating the luxury of being able to go into the pub for a drink and being able to sleep in a proper bed. He knew how much he looked forward to Brian's visits and how much he appreciated being able to talk with someone other than himself. On a few occasions he even made the long walk back to the town at night for no other reason than to look at the lights in windows and to think of people doing all the things that he would have liked to have been doing.

He was only metres from where the track joined with the track leading down to the hut when he saw two young men coming along the track from the road. He contemplated retreating into the bush, but one of them indicated that he had seen him, wishing him good morning as he did so. Shane decided that he had no option other than to step out on to the track and acknowledge the greeting. He was no linguist, but from the boy's accent he guessed that he was from somewhere else.

'Danish? German?' he asked after returning the greeting.

'German,' said the youth, turning around so that Shane could see the German flag on the back of his pack.

Shane smiled and, with a sweeping gesture that took in the bush around him, asked, 'So, might one ask what you are doing here in the middle of nowhere?'

The young man with the flag, who introduced himself as Friedrich, said that he and his friend were hoping to get a lift south, but they had not been having any luck, and when they saw the track they decided to take a short break. He also said that he was having trouble with his backpack, and he wanted to see if he could possibly fix it.

When Shane looked at the pack, he could see that a number of teeth in the main zip fastener had broken. He shook his head, handing it back to Friedrich, and said, 'Not much to be done here, I'm afraid.' Then he thought for a moment and added, 'But, then again, I might be able to help you... ' He remembered that he had a good, almost new, backpack in the cave, one that Brian had once brought in filled with supplies. He really had no use for it, and he was sure that Brian would understand.

He said that he was camping nearby and that he had a spare backpack. If he was interested, he was more than welcome to it. Friedrich looked at his friend, who had introduced himself as Hans, and the two boys spoke briefly with each other in German. They were obviously a bit wary, even suspicious, but they said that they could wait.

Shane nodded. He did not want the boys following him, so he plunged into the bush on the opposite side of the track and then worked his way around in a half circle until he was on his way to the caves. When he arrived back with the backpack thirty minutes later he was surprised to see Brian sitting and talking with the boys. He had forgotten that Brian was driving to Canberra and that he had said he would drop off supplies on his way.

The backpack was perfect.

Friedrich wanted to pay Shane, but he refused. The boy emptied his backpack and moved most things over to the new pack. There were a few bits and pieces that he decided he no longer wanted, including a scarf that had obviously passed its use-by date, and he left them in the old pack. He would have liked to have taken his flag, but it had been firmly sewn on to the pack. After a few attempts to break the stitching, he gave up and shook hands with Shane.

There was nothing to discuss about the lift: the boys were going south, Brian was travelling in the same direction, and he had plenty of room in the car. Brian and the two Germans waved Shane goodbye, then Shane removed a couple of things from the backpack that he felt he might have use for, pushed the damaged backpack behind a rock and, shouldering the two bags of supplies, returned to the cave.

He had meant to come back and collect the backpack, but, as often happens, other things managed to come in between, and he forgot all about it.

26

Three weeks after Evans went missing, his body was found at the bottom of the ridge. He had fallen more than one hundred metres down the side of the escarpment, and the doctor who later examined the remains was quite certain that death would have been instantaneous. The body would probably have lain hidden among the dense understorey of bracken fern for months or even years but for a dog belonging to a man called John.

John worked on one of the properties on the flat, and on this particular day, he was driving along the road at the bottom of the ridge on his way home. Almost level with the place where Evans' body had fallen, he got a flat tyre. He stopped his truck, removed the spare from the back and set about changing the wheel. While he was working, his dog, who normally rode in the back of his truck, ran backwards and forwards along the edge of the road, delighting in the unexpected freedom. After some minutes, the dog ventured further afield, and then, as John was loading the damaged wheel on to the truck, it began to bark.

John did not react at first, thinking that the dog had probably found a rabbit burrow or something similar, but the barking continued, and John left the truck to find out what was the matter.

He called to the dog, but the dog did not take any

notice, and finally John pushed his way through the waist-high ferns.

***

Dave Bennett and a couple of colleagues from one of the Sydney offices called around to Greg's sister's house to reinterview Greg. As they stepped out of the car, Dave reflected on the fact that it was the beginning of spring, and that there was a feeling of cool optimism in the air. He was also thinking about the short conversation he had had with Gregory Payne when he rang and told him that he needed to interview him again. When he explained that there was a chance he was once again the prime suspect in a possible murder case, Greg had sounded surprised and nervous but not particularly guilt-ridden. As Dave rang the doorbell, he wondered what it was he had missed in the first interview.

After the initial introductions, he came straight to the point and asked if Greg knew that his wife was planning to leave him. Greg seemed confused. 'Was she? That's certainly more than I knew,' he remarked while everyone took a seat in the beautifully furnished but rather formal lounge room.

As the interview proceeded, Dave began to seriously wonder if Greg's sister may have misunderstood her sister-in-law's intentions. Greg claimed no knowledge of Sandra's plans to leave him: as far as he was concerned their relationship had been extremely positive. They loved each other; there was no reason why Sandra would have wanted to leave him. When Dave suggested that she may have found someone else, Greg became angry and refused to answer any more questions.

Needing confirmation of what had been said on the

phone, Dave then spoke with Greg's sister who merely repeated what she had already told him: Sandra had met someone else and she was planning to leave Greg. 'I always had a lot of time for Sandra,' she added, 'she was a genuinely nice girl, but I think she was very lonely – Greg was away so much with his work. She never complained, but, you know how it is... it's a, how would you say, a *discontentment*; it's always there, blocking out everything else. She once told me that she desperately wanted to start a family, but Greg wanted to wait. But, let's face it, there's a limit to how long you can wait, isn't there?' She paused for a moment, and then she said, 'I know he's my brother, and I do love him, but I have to be honest with you: he is very controlling. I'm sure Sandra loved him, as least she did once, but I think she had reached a point where she just wanted to be free.

'If you believe that something terrible happened to Sandra, I know for sure that Greg could not have been involved; he's just not that type of person. My guess is that nothing of the sort happened. Sandra simply left him.'

Dave wondered about *he's just not that type of person*, and he asked himself just what type of person would kill his or her partner: the answer, as far as he was concerned, was just about anyone. After taking Greg's laptop, they drove to Greg's home and collected his computer. Dave noticed the book lying next to the computer, *Virtual Reality and Abstract Truth* by V. A. Collins. He picked it up and leafed through it, but deciding that it had absolutely nothing to do with the case he left it lying on the table.

***

Finally Detective Senior Constable Bennett had to admit that there was absolutely no case against Greg. There was no body and Greg adamantly refused to accept the idea that Sandra intended to leave him. The forensic experts trawled through the electronic devices without finding anything that showed that Greg was lying. As far as Greg was concerned, he and Sandra loved each other, and Sandra had simply disappeared.

In desperation, Dave phoned Vincent and asked for his perspective, even his advice.

Vincent said, 'But it's obvious, Bennett.'

The detective was taken aback. 'What do you mean, *obvious*?'

'Greg is living in different realities. Remember when he visited you, and he claimed that Sandra was not missing?'

Dave interrupted. 'Now *that* was really weird; I mean, he was in hospital... '

Vincent continued, 'Yes, it was weird, but we only understand a very small fraction of the mind's capabilities. It is not impossible to be in two places at once; the thing that really amazes me is that he was able to pull other people into his own self-deception.

'When Greg turned up here or, we should probably say, an image of Greg turned up here, it was a reflection of Greg's mind telling him that everything was okay; everything was exactly the way it had always been. It was how he *wanted* things to be. The same thing happened when Sandra disappeared. It is very possible that he knew that she was leaving him - perhaps she told him, or perhaps he suspected it - but it really does not matter how he knew or thought he knew, his brain refused to accept it. When she disappeared, he was extremely distressed. She had been taken away from him. He, in many ways, became the victim.

'As a victim, Greg was able to retain his belief that everything was as it always had been. When he allowed himself to admit that Sandra was no longer in the picture, he was still able to hang on to the belief that were she to be found then everything would again revert to normal.

'It is Greg's idea of *normal* that is at the bottom of all of this.' Vincent paused for a moment, and then he said, 'Remember what he said about the connections being at the far end of the threads; if he had fully understood this, he may have been able to accept the fact that there was something at the end of Sandra's thread that propelled her into a situation where she "went missing".

'He couldn't understand it, because in reality he did not want to. I know I've said it so many times,' Vincent continued, 'but everything is connected; nothing happens in isolation. Reality can be virtual, but it can also be abstract. In Greg's case, it was a bit of both.'

Bennett remembered the book lying next to the computer. He began to ask, 'That book *Virtual Reality and Abstract Truth...* ' but Vincent Tyler was no longer on the line.

***

No one ever found out exactly what happened to Sandra Payne. Her sister-in-law continued to insist that she had met someone else and that she had been intending to leave her husband for some time. 'I think he may have been from Canada,' she had said when Dave questioned her for the third or fourth time, 'but, of course, I could be wrong; I never actually met him.'

Greg, on the other hand, insisted that everything between himself and his wife had been just perfect. Obviously she had been abducted and possibly murdered; it was just a matter of finding the person who did it. Dave had listened to Vincent's theories about different realities, and he really wanted to believe him, but even as he stamped the case file as closed something was still niggling him. He conjured up the image of Sandra and Greg walking out to the ridge, and Sandra suddenly turning to Greg and telling him that she was leaving him and why. Did Greg simply ignore the information and step into a reality where everything was as it had always been, or did he become angry and lose his temper? Did Greg kill his wife and hide the body where no one had thought to look?

Dave wanted to accept the theory about different realities, but he still had his reservations. If a body were suddenly to turn up, he would have a pretty good idea who it was and who was responsible.

***

The detective had no reason not to believe Shane's account of having met the two German boys on the track and of Brian having driven them to Canberra. They had told Shane that they were hoping to reach Perth, and a new investigation showed that they had managed to pick up a lift from Canberra with a semi-trailer driver going to Mildura. In Mildura the trail suddenly ran dry, and though the police questioned hundreds of truck drivers they were unable to find out where the boys went next.

Six months after Shane had come forward, and Evans' body had been discovered at the bottom of the cliff, a semi-trailer driver, crossing the Nullabor on the Eyre Highway, stopped for a short break about thirty kilometres east of Border Village. He had been driving for eight hours straight. He pulled over to the side of the road, drank the remainder of the coffee that was in his thermos and then took a short walk away from the road to stretch his legs.

The flat ground was covered with saltbush, blue bush and, in parts, yellow grass and the odd stunted tree. He lit a cigarette and stood for a while, watching several kangaroos hopping across the plain and then began walking back to his truck. It was at this moment that his foot struck against something under the sand. When he bent down to see what it was, he saw that it was a skull. When he dug away some of the sand, he found a pile of bones and another skull.

The DNA tests showed that the remains definitely belonged to the two Germans, but whether or not they had died of natural causes was impossible to ascertain. The boys' backpacks, very much deteriorated, were found close by, covered by sand, and though there were no marks on the skeletons that indicated violence the possibility could not be completely ruled out. The suggestion that the two boys had been hitch-hiking and had been dropped somewhere along the long stretch of road did not make any sense – there was no reason why anyone would have left them in the middle of nowhere and then continued driving west. No one could work out why the boys had been on foot, but it was obvious that they had been. Several investigators, ignoring all the things that did not make sense, decided that the only possibility was the one where the boys had been dropped off, failed to pick up a second lift and consequently died from lack of water and food; however there were several who were firmly convinced that the boys had been brutally murdered, though how or why no one had any idea.

Dave felt that both explanations reeked of melodrama, and he felt a sense of failure in not being able to pinpoint exactly what had happened. At the same time, he could not stop thinking about what Vincent had said about the umbrella connection, and he wondered just how far the connection reached.

***

A couple of weeks after Shane had been found, Thelma phoned Dave Bennett and said that she had heard from Betsy. She was alive and well. The story that Dave was finally able to piece together after speaking with Thelma on the phone, and then asking her to come into the station to make an official statement, was definitely not what anyone had imagined.

Betsy's car *did* break down, and because there was no mobile coverage she had then walked further along the road, hoping to find a spot from where she could make a call. Completely focused on her phone, she did not at first notice the small blue hatchback with the Victorian number plates that had pulled up alongside her. The driver, a white-haired gentleman somewhere around her age, rolled down the window on the passenger side and asked her if she needed help. Betsy answered that her car had broken down and that she had no mobile coverage.

The gentleman then asked her if she would like a lift. She thought for a couple of seconds: there was not much point waiting on the side of the road for help when it might not even turn up; once she reached her destination she could always phone Thelma. She told the man where she was going before the car had broken down (omitting the planned detour via her sister's place), and he said that he would be driving through the very town she had intended to visit and that he could easily drop her there.

Betsy had hesitated but only briefly. Accepting a lift would be so completely and utterly out of character for her, but just for once she wanted to be out of character. Just for once she wanted to be someone else, someone who did things on the spur of the moment. She had always done what others had told her to do: first her parents, then her husband and, of late, her sister. She knew that there was a possibility that she might be making her life's biggest mistake, but something about the man told her that this possibility was very slight.

During the drive, it became obvious that Betsy and the man, whose name was Arthur, had a lot in common. They were, as she had guessed, almost the same age, and Arthur had lost his wife a year ago, about the same time that Betsy became a widow. They both loved classical music, enjoyed Scandinavian noir and voted for the same political party. Although Betsy had lived most of her life inland, she had a special liking for the ocean, and Arthur lived only minutes from the Great Southern Ocean. Most of all, they were both very lonely.

When they reached the small town, Arthur had asked her where she would like him to drop her, but having taken the first step, Betsy was prepared to go even further: she would take an enormous gamble on a new reality. She had looked at Arthur and smiled as she placed her hand on his. 'I'd love to see that wonderful house of yours by the sea,' she said.

Over the next few months, Betsy's new reality slowly took shape. She reverted to her original name, Elizabeth, and instead of using her married name, she used her maiden name, Hamilton. After six months, Arthur and Elizabeth were married in a simple civil ceremony, and Betsy, now Elizabeth, had never been happier.

Occasionally she had twinges of conscience about what she had done, and she did miss her sister, but she knew that part of accepting her new life was being able to forget about the old. She was quite sure that Thelma would never accept what she had done, and she did not want guilt to cloud her new-found happiness.

Almost two years after Betsy had gone missing, she and Arthur had cause to drive north into New South Wales. As they had business in the same area as the town, Betsy decided, on the spur of the moment, to phone Thelma. She tried twice, but when her sister answered, she had no idea what she should say, and she hung up. However, on their return to Victoria, she summoned up all her courage and she made the call she should have made two years earlier.

Thelma was shocked, unbelieving, furious, ecstatic, emotional, angry, upset and angry all over again. How could Betsy have done such a thing to her? Betsy, now Elizabeth, had no answer; all she could say was that she was radiantly happy.

After the sisters had talked for well over an hour, Thelma, who would never have dared step outside of her own reality, began to have the slightest inkling of what Betsy was trying to say. In between tears, the two women were finally reconciled with promises on both sides to visit, as soon as possible, and to catch up on all the time lost.

Dave Bennett knew that Betsy Riley should have been arrested for wasting police time, but he decided that her story was the one ray of light in the case of the missing people, and he simply stamped her file closed and packed it away with the others.

***

Vincent Tyler opened the door to his small harbour-side unit. He walked through to the lounge room with the large window overlooking the water, poured himself a drink and sat down on the white leather sofa. In many ways the last twelve months had been difficult, but he had learnt much. About himself and about others. He had learnt even more about the different kinds of reality.

One reality of a slightly different kind was the gold that had belonged to his grandfather and now belonged to him. He was not a monetary person, and he would have been quite happy for Shane to have retained everything that he had found. As far as Vincent was concerned, anyone who had spent six years in the wilderness, had certainly earned it. But the law insisted, and Shane and Brian were happy to be able to divide the remainder between themselves.

Though, from what Vincent was given to understand, the gold paled in comparison with Shane's relief when Dave Bennett arrested Shane's nemesis who, as it turned out, was wanted elsewhere for both intimidation and extortion. Due to the complexities surrounding the case, Shane fortunately managed to avoid a gaol sentence, and, placed on a good behaviour bond, he set about putting the last few years behind him and getting his life back on track.

Vincent's thoughts moved from Shane to Greg. He was

still not completely sure about Greg, even though the man had been right about the connections all being at the other end. Vincent wondered if Greg's insight had had anything to do with the fact that he himself was split between several realities. He wondered whether this was still the case and whether Greg would ever be able to anchor himself to just one reality, the reality of Sandra's disappearance. Occasionally, Vincent found himself wondering, like Bennett, if Greg actually knew more about the disappearance than he was prepared to let on.

He watched some yachts beating across the water, then he finished his drink and stood up. He collected his suitcase from where he had left it standing in the hall and wheeled it into the centre of the room. He lay it down on the floor and unzipped the main zip fastener.

Then he opened the lid and looked inside.

Acknowledgements

Many thanks to Ruth, for reading the manuscript and for her most welcome advice and support, and to Annette, for all her practical help and suggestions with the cover.

www.ingramcontent.com/pod-product-compliance
Lightning Source LLC
Chambersburg PA
CBHW050324110726
47899CB00007B/2364